About the Author
The Tudor Maid

Elizabeth Kelly is the author of Household: A Post-Pandemic Story set in the fictional future. The Tudor Maid is her first historical novel. She enjoys travelling to see places of historical interest including the Pyramids, the Great Wall of China and the medieval abbeys of Yorkshire.

THE TUDOR MAID

AUTHOR: ELIZABETH KELLY

ILLUSTRATOR: JULIA BAI

Illustrator: Julia Bai

Contents

List of Characters in The Tudor Maid: Fictional

Mistress Margery Hallows: Royal dressmaker to Queen Anne, the Lady Anne of Cleves and Queen Elizabeth I.
Master John Hallows: Farmer on the Hever estate.
Mistress Carew: The housekeeper of Hever Castle.
Mistress Harvey: The mistress of the seamstresses.
Mary Dacre: A court seamstress.
Nan Cobham: A court seamstress.

List of Characters in The Tudor Maid: Historical

King Henry VIII.
Queen Catherine of Aragon.
Mistress Anne Boleyn: Queen of England 1533 – 1536.
Queen Jane Seymour.
Lady Anne of Cleves.
Queen Mary I.
Queen Elizabeth I.

Sir Thomas Boleyn.
Lady Elizabeth Boleyn.
Mistress Mary Boleyn.
Sir George Boleyn.
Lord Henry Percy.
Sir Thomas Wyatt.
Sir William Carey.
Master William Stafford.
Master Mark Smeaton: A court musician.
Sir Henry Norris.
Sir Francis Weston.

Sir William Brereton.
Thomas Percy: A courtier.
Edmund Chapuys: The Spanish Ambassador.

Cardinal Thomas Wolsey.
Master Thomas Cromwell.
Sir William Cecil: Councillor to Queen Elizabeth I.
Sir Thomas Parry: Treasurer to Queen Elizabeth I.
Sir Robert Dudley: Master of the Horse to Queen Elizabeth I.

Lady Margaret Lee: The Mistress of the Wardrobe to Queen Anne.
Mistress Margaret Shelton: Lady in Waiting to Queen Anne.
Mistress Elizabeth Browne: Lady in Waiting to Queen Anne.
Mistress Mary Orchard: Former nurse to Queen Anne.
Father Matthew Parker: Chaplain to Queen Anne.
Master William Cornish: The Master of the Revels to the king.
Master Hans Holbein: A court artist.
Master Cornelius Hayes: The King's goldsmith.
Sir William Kingston: The Constable of the Tower of London.

Mistress Catherine Ashley: The Mistress of the Wardrobe to Queen Elizabeth.
Master John Ashley: The Keeper of the Jewel House.
Mistress Blanche Parry: The Keeper of the Queen's Books.
Lady Mary Sidney: Lady in Waiting to Queen Elizabeth.
Lady Dorothy Stafford: Lady in Waiting to Queen Elizabeth.
Father Jonas Wheeler: Chaplain to Queen Elizabeth.
Sir Thomas Benger: The Master of the Revels to the Queen.
Master David Smyth and Master William Middleton: The Queen's Broderers.
Mistress Alice Montague: The Queen's silk woman.
Master Robert Brandon: The Queen's goldsmith.
Master Nicholas Hilliard: An apprentice goldsmith.

Notes on the Tudor Maid

1 Queen Anne Boleyn had a maid named Margery Horsman, who worked in the Queen's Wardrobe. Margery became Anne's maid of honour in 1532 and she was one of the ladies who attended her coronation in 1533.

2 Margery Horsman visited Queen Anne at the Tower of London and brought her some items of clothes including six frontlets (decorative bands worn with French hoods) in May 1536.

3 Lady Margaret Lee, the Mistress of the Robes to Queen Anne, retired from court in 1536 rather than serve her successor Queen Jane.

4 Henry VIII gave Hever Castle to Lady Anne of Cleves as part of the settlement following the annulment of their marriage in 1540.

5 Lady Anne of Cleves requested the Princess Elizabeth to take into her service one of her maids named Dorothy Curzon in her last will and testament written on 12th July 1557.

6 Queen Elizabeth I was served by two male broderers named David Smyth and William Middleton. In 1569 they entered into a dispute over the division of work which was settled by David Smyth taking responsibility for making the Queen's gowns and William Middleton embroidering the royal furnishings.

Introduction

Slowly, I unwrap the green silk bindings of the pear-shaped lute as I do each year on the anniversary of 17th May. It is all that I have left to remind me of my great love. I remember how beautifully he used to play and sing his love songs. But always for her – never for me. I remind myself that I am only the humble servant of a once-great household that has now sadly fallen low. But once I lived a life of verve and excitement in the highest circle of the land. I served my lady in the royal court of England. I was present when she was raised up to be the queen. And I was there three years later when she was imprisoned in the Tower. Surely now you can guess her name?

I am now an old woman of seventy, but I well remember my youth at the court of old King Henry. I have never before told my secrets to anyone, but now all those who might have been interested are long dead. Only fools told of what they knew at court, yet surprisingly there were many who could not resist the fleeting pleasures of boasting and gossip despite the risks. Only now that we are living in the reign of Good Queen Bess is it safe for me to admit that I knew her mother, the unfortunate Queen Anne.

CHAPTER 1:
HEVER CASTLE, KENT (1520)

My name is Margery Hallows and I was born the sixth child of a poor farmer on the great estate of Hever in Kent. My mother died young and so I learned hardship and industry as soon as I could walk. My older sisters taught me how to bake bread and brew good ale, to milk the cow and fatten the poultry. It was expected that one day I would become the capable wife of a hardworking farmer. But my destiny followed a different path because of the great gift which my grandmother Hallows gave me. She was a skilled needlewoman who taught me how to knit and sew at an early age. As the youngest in the family, I was small-statured and rather plain in looks. My eyes were hazel and my hair was brown and perfectly straight. I wasn't someone at whom you would look twice. My best features were my hands. Small and fine, they were adept at any task. I could turn a spindle with only one hand as I went about the house. By the age of seven I could hem sheets, knit gloves and darn stockings better than many a grown woman. As these were profitable skills they released me from the drudgery of cleaning, baking and laundering. Unfortunately, this set me apart from my brothers and sisters who resented my easier lot in the household. "Betty-by-the-fireside" they named me in derision, for naturally I worked where there was good light. My father never beat me like the others for he was afraid of causing damage. As I grew older, I learned the art of embroidery and how to cut out and fit patterns for clothes. And this led to the next step of my fortune.

My father was justified when word of my gifts came to the attention of the castle steward. I was just ten when Mistress Carew sent for my father and spoke for me. She was the housekeeper at Hever Castle and had served both Sir William Boleyn and his son Sir Thomas. She wanted a young assistant to care for the household linen.

Normally a premium would be paid for a place in a noble house, but my father had a reputation for being long-headed and driving a hard bargain. In my case, he received a payment in silver coins for he knew my skills were valuable. In addition, I was provided with a set of new clothes suitable for my life as a household servant. I arrived at the castle wearing a white linen cap, a black dress with a white neckerchief and apron, and a pair of black woollen stockings. Most remarkably of all, I wore my first pair of shoes with buckles to fasten them instead of wooden clogs on my feet. My father gave me his blessing and told me to mind my manners and do as I was bid. I could tell that he was pleased to have settled me in life so early and so advantageously. I felt that I had left my childhood behind and entered a woman's estate. Surely this offered me a better future than marriage to a farm labourer like my two older sisters. And so I left behind the privations of my father's house for the life of a skilled seamstress in the noble household of the Boleyn's.

Life in the castle was indeed a step up from our simple farmhouse. The castle itself reminded me of stories of King Arthur's Camelot with its fine glazed windows and a moat surrounded by lawns and gardens. Mistress Carew established me in the household and tried to better me in every way. The other servants called me Mistress Sparrow because I was small, brown and quiet like a hedge-sparrow. But Mistress Carew treated me like a daughter and praised me for my "golden hands." She made rather a pet of me for I think she felt guilty about taking me from my family so young. I soon moved beyond plain sewing and mending and was entrusted to sew shirts for Sir Thomas and embroider bedlinen for Lady Elizabeth. I looked forward to many industrious and happy years in this household. I thought that I would remain there all my life and perhaps marry another servant one day. In time, I might even succeed my good mistress as the housekeeper.

CHAPTER 2:

Mistress Anne (1522)

But when I turned twelve my life unexpectedly changed again. In 1522 Mistress Anne, the youngest daughter of Sir Thomas, returned to England from service at the court of Queen Claude of France. I had once overheard Sir Thomas and Lady Elizabeth discussing their plans for their children. "They have the best educations to prepare them for life at court and noble marriages. Anne especially, for her service at the French court has given her accomplishments far beyond her English contemporaries. I have high hopes for her!" The first time I saw her I was struck by her poise and sophistication for a girl of only fifteen. She was only my height, but she carried herself so confidently that it only added to her charm. She was not a classical beauty, but her magnetic charm and force of personality were irresistible. She seemed in awe of no-one except her formidable mother, Lady Elizabeth. My grandmother Hallows had been reckoned wise for she knew many receipts and remedies, could brew and preserve and had a repertoire of songs, rhymes and old stories. I admired the measured competence of Mistress Carew whose knowledge far surpassed that of any of the farmers or their wives. But Mistress Anne seemed to me like an exotic princess in a fable. She had been educated in a foreign court to read and write like a learned clerk and sing and play like a troubadour.

My first meeting with Mistress Anne was as Mistress Carew's assistant in fitting her for a new gown. At first she did not condescend to notice me, but once the costume was completed to her satisfaction she insisted that I should be appointed as her personal maid. It was one of the keys to her character that she wanted only the best for herself. "Nobody in England is familiar with the new French fashions, but I could teach Margery," she persuaded her mother. So it was agreed that I would make her dresses. She did not make me her confidant – no-one was ever that close – but she shared with me her desire to outshine the noble ladies of England. So from the beginning I knew that she was ambitious. In the service of Mistress Anne I also became acquainted with her barbed tongue.

"Do you know how to make lace, Margery?"

"No, Mistress Anne. It is not much practiced hereabouts. I believe your parents get their ruffs from London."

"They come from Flanders, Margery. What a pity you haven't the skill."

I discovered that Mistress Anne enjoyed boasting about her life in the French court. Naturally, she could not brag in front of her parents without receiving a sharp rebuke so she would reminisce to me instead.

"I expect Hever Castle seems like a paradise to you, Margery."

"Oh yes, Mistress Anne."

"But then you grew up on a farm. You cannot imagine what I have seen in the French court. All the ladies wore the finest clothes and they changed their appearance every day. Not like the ladies of England who wear the same dress for a week at a time. In France an ignorant girl like you would only be allowed to mend shifts!"

Then she would dart a sly look at me to see if I dared to take offence. But I always took care to keep my eyes downcast before Mistress Anne. "Yes, my lady," I murmured.

"Yes, my lady," she mimicked back. "No wonder they call you Mistress Sparrow. All you can do is cheep at your betters. You can return to your mending now."

I made a bob. "Thank you, my lady."

However, the welcome news came that an alliance was planned with her Irish cousin, James Butler, the Earl of Ormonde, and this greatly improved the mood of Mistress Anne. She took to riding and dancing in the mornings and reading poetry and playing love songs on her lute in the afternoons. I was instructed to prepare her wardrobe for her marriage. She liked to appear unconscious of her appearance when every stitch of her costume had been planned with meticulous care. I did my utmost to meet her exacting standards and she grew to trust my judgement, although she rarely praised my efforts.

Several months later Mistress Carew told me that there would be no marriage to Lord Butler. Instead, Mistress Anne would be going to the royal court to be a maid of honour to Queen Catherine of Aragon. I would accompany her there as her personal tirewoman. It would be my responsibility to make her the most fashionable dresses at the most reasonable cost. You can imagine my astonishment and my pride at this news. I would not only travel to London but see the royal court itself. I was too young to appreciate the dangers of royal service. I saw only the glamour which surrounded the lives of the courtiers and thought myself the most fortunate girl in England. On the farm we lived according to the steady rhythm of the agricultural year. But at the royal palaces we lived in an endless cycle of pageants in which each one was more impressive than before. It would be my role to ensure that Mistress Anne would stand out from the other ladies in waiting and be admired for the style of her dress. I hoped that I would be equal to the task and not fail her expectations.

CHAPTER 3:

THE ROYAL COURT (FEBRUARY 1523)

On our arrival at the palace Mistress Anne was escorted to the quarters of the ladies-in-waiting and I was directed to the servants' dormitory. I was overwhelmed by the size of York Place which was many times larger than Hever Castle. In my ignorance I had thought that this was the London residence of the king and queen, but I soon discovered that this was the property of Cardinal Wolsey, the great Lord Chancellor of England. The king owned over sixty houses, but only five of the royal palaces could accommodate the whole of the court including Greenwich, Woodstock, Beaulieu, Richmond and Eltham. During the summer months, the king and queen went on progresses around the kingdom to show themselves to the common people in which they were accompanied by only half of the court. There was invariably great contention amongst the royal servants over which of them would have the honour to be included in their retinue.

My duties began the following day when I was introduced to Lady Margaret Lee, the Mistress of the Queen's Robes. The sewing rooms of the royal court were great storehouses of the best fabrics in the land so that they resembled the fabled treasure-cave of Aladdin. Some of them were so valuable that they were kept under lock and key and were a constant source of anxiety to Lady Lee. She wrote detailed inventories for the personal attention of the queen and maintained a constant vigilance against theft and waste. I was constantly chided, "Take care, girl. That piece of velvet is worth more than a year's wages!" Fortunately, Lady Lee was a neighbour of the Boleyn family and allowed all the resources of the sewing room to be made available to me in creating Mistress Anne's costumes. However, I was firmly reminded that only those of royal rank were allowed to wear cloth of gold, purple silk or ermine fur in their gowns.

Mistress Anne was as dazzled as I, but she pretended indifference. "Tis not so fine as the silk of France," she would sniff.

The head seamstress was Mistress Harvey and she had served in the court since the days of the king's father. She supervised the work and conduct of the seamstresses and made sure that we were modest and diligent. I had hoped that she would be as kind to me as Mistress Carew, but she was inclined to put on airs like many of the servants at the court. There was just as much rivalry below the salt as above it. At first, she was inclined to dismiss a country girl like me with a Kentish accent and was put out when it was made clear that I was the personal dressmaker of the Boleyn's. However, her attitude changed once she recognised the superior style of Mistress Anne, although a mere knight's daughter. It was assumed that I had served her in France and had a thorough knowledge of their court fashions.

The other seamstresses had also served at court for many years and were much older than I. At first, they were inclined to treat me as an apprentice until they saw that my skills were a match for them. But they were pleased to have an opportunity to show off their knowledge of the court to a newcomer. At night in the dormitory, when they were away from the scrutiny of Mistress Harvey, they would tell scandalous stories about the nobility of the court. And so I learned that only the previous year the great Duke of Buckingham had been beheaded for plotting against the throne. I was assured that King Henry was the greatest king in Christendom and his court was the finest in the world. And when it came to Queen Catherine all the women of the sewing room universally sang her praises. "The Queen is greatly loved." "She is gracious and welcoming to all." "A devout and charitable lady who is a good influence on the court." "She is a generous mistress who takes care of her servants." "Your young mistress is fortunate to be one of her ladies in waiting."

I was curious to know what Mistress Anne would say about the Queen. So the next morning, I went early to her bedroom bringing a pincushion on a loop of ribbon which was an indispensable item for a lady in waiting. She accepted it graciously and I could see that she was in a good mood.

"Have you met the Queen, Mistress Anne?" I ventured to ask.

"I was presented to her Majesty yesterday," she preened. "She was kind enough to call me a pretty little courtier and said that she hoped I would be happy at the court. Perhaps today she will ask me to read or sing for her. But now it is time for me to attend morning chapel."

As the weeks passed, I learned more about Queen Catherine. Her life was like a story out of a fairy tale. Born a princess of Spain she was married at fifteen to Prince Arthur Tudor, widowed at sixteen and then remarried to King Henry at the age of twenty-three. They had six children together, but sadly only their daughter, the Princess Mary, had lived. She could speak many languages, her motto was, "humble and loyal," and she was greatly admired for her piety, diplomacy and good example. I wondered if the benevolence of Queen Catherine would make Mistress Anne more demure. But life at court generally rewarded the ambitious rather than the virtuous. Mistress Anne was biding her time to make her mark. The court was her best chance to make a good match. Her older sister Mary was already married to Sir William Carey, one of the king's courtiers. But what the other seamstresses did not like to tell me was that it was common knowledge in the court that Mary Boleyn was receiving marked attentions from the king.

I was impatient to see the king and my chance came soon. The month after our arrival both Mary and Anne were chosen to take part in the Chateau Vert masque as part of the Shrovetide celebrations. In the Great Chamber of York Place a green castle was erected to stage a play on the theme of unrequited love. Mary played the part of Kindness and Anne played the role of Perseverance. I was immediately set to work to make their special costumes of white satin embroidered with gold thread. The festivities began with a jousting tournament in which Henry rode out with the motto *"Elle mon coeur a navera,"* (She has wounded my heart) clearly embroidered on the trappings of his horse. That evening after the pageant Henry made his meaning clear by partnering Mary in the court dances. I had persuaded Mistress Harvey to let me stand at the back of the hall in case the dresses should need attention. And so I had my first sight of the great King Harry. He was a giant of a man with flaming red hair and resplendent jewels. The evening was a complete success and Mary was acknowledged as the established favourite of the king. No one even noticed that it was Mistress Anne's first public appearance at court.

CHAPTER 4:

THE BETROTHAL (1523)

Mistress Anne was born for the life of the court. She was a high accomplished woman who was expert in the language and manners of France. She could make witty conversation, knew all the English dances and could sing "like a second Orpheus." She could accompany herself on the lute and play the flute and the virginals. Her talent, youth and beauty made her an ornament of the court and she appeared in almost all the masques. In the end I grew to dread the gaudy pageants for every costume meant hours of extra work. Often there would be last-minute alterations which required me to sew all night by candlelight. Lady Lee lamented the waste of good candles, but they were the least of my concerns. No-one ever troubled about a servant's loss of sleep. We were expected to serve at any hour of the day or night and were frequently reminded of our good fortune in having a place at court. And there were perquisites to be gained such as valuable castoffs from the wardrobe and New Year's gifts. All the young women were avidly saving for their dowries for how else would we get a husband? The young serving men were all looking to make a match with a woman of property, preferably a widow of comfortable means who did not need to marry to please her family. There was always the hope that our mistresses might arrange suitable matches for us. It was considered part of their duty towards their servants. Mistress Harvey would often tease me by saying that I must look about and make the most of my chances or else I would end up back on the farm in Kent.

We often wondered what matches our ladies would make and would whisper together whenever Mistress Hervey left the room. I had no doubt that the Boleyn family would negotiate a fine marriage for Mistress Anne. Perhaps with an English lord or a French nobleman. I dreamed that I would accompany her and make fine wardrobes for every occasion. I didn't care to confide in the others for they liked to mock me at every opportunity. "You'll end up in Scotland dressed in blankets and eating porridge!" I knew that they were jealous of my lady's success. However, they were much better informed than I for it was from them that I learned of my lady's partiality for Lord Henry Percy. He was the son of the Earl of Northumberland and one of the greatest heirs in the land. I heard that he was desperate to marry her, but nothing came of the match as Mistress Anne had no fortune. It seemed folly to me since he had more than enough fortune for both of them. Cardinal Wolsey warned Lord Percy that in seeking his own match he had not only offended his father, but also his sovereign. Finally, he married the heiress Mary Talbot but was deeply unhappy for he never forgot his deep love for Anne. If only they had married when they had the chance then it would have prevented so much tragedy!

After Mistress Anne's betrothal to Henry Percy was broken off she was sent back to Hever Castle for a season. Mistress Anne was furious with anger and grief and blamed the Cardinal for his interference. But I was delighted to return to the familiar happy scenes of Hever again.

"Why don't you go to visit your family, Margery?"

"My father would not want the cost of boarding me, Mistress Anne. If there is any urgent news I will hear it from the Castle Steward."

I gladly undertook an inventory of the household linen for Mistress Carew. But Mistress Anne was sadly discomposed by the loss of her suitor and her exile from court. She no longer troubled to change her costume every day, nor practice her dancing and music. Instead, she would ride out with her grooms every day and return home exhausted. Finally, the Lady Elizabeth intervened.

"Really Anne, this cannot continue day after day. You must vary your activities. You could attend my meetings with the steward and housekeeper and learn how to manage a household."

"As you wish, mother," she replied evenly.

"We must all adjust ourselves on our return from the court. Think of it as a rest."

"I had as lief never go back to court."

"For such as us, there is only the court. You are young and have many years ahead of you. Your accomplishments will keep. But you must find a suitable occupation for yourself. Unless you want others to pity you."

"There is plenty for me to do here, mother. I shall willingly stay at home tomorrow."

Fortunately, the next day a welcome visitor arrived. It was their good friend Sir Thomas Wyatt who lived on the neighbouring estate of Allington. I was told that he was a famous poet who was greatly admired at the English court. He and Mistress Anne spent the entire day walking in the gardens and talking together in the library. On his departure Mistress Anne announced her plan to take up a course of reading in the mornings. She spent her days at home making a collection of her favourite poems. Sir Thomas visited her again and afterwards she decided to undertake a more ambitious project. She sent for me and set me to knitting worsted stockings while she discussed how the revels of the English court did not compare with those of France.

"I will write a masque that is worthy of the Tudor court. The Master of the Revels, William Cornish, knows nothing of the classics. He is only interested in planning decorations to match the costumes. His masques are all of a piece. Each time there is the same routine of dancing and singing. The Chateau Vert pageant was a contrast between the virtues and the vices. It was no better than a morality play. What the court needs is a real spectacle in which all the parts fit together as a whole." This plan kept Anne occupied for many weeks as she selected the theme and planned her material. "It shall be The Judgement of Paris between the goddesses Hera, Athena and Aphrodite. The king shall play Paris and choose the most beautiful one of the three. And the goddesses shall each make rhymed speeches in favour of power, wisdom and love. There will be songs and music on each of these qualities. Finally, Paris will declare that love is greater than power or wisdom. Then there will be celebrations and dances on Love Triumphant followed by a banquet."

I would have liked to have seen this masque. But when Mistress Anne was summoned back to court, the project was somehow forgotten. The ladies in waiting were far too busy to organise court entertainments. It was enough for them to keep their mistress comfortable and diverted. And so the Master of the Revels was left to plan his masques according to his own notions. He had a great liking for old legends and courtly romances such as the Green Knight. I always found them enchanting, but Mistress Anne was harder to please.

CHAPTER 5:
A Theme of Courtly Love (1524-1525)

One of her greatest triumphs was the occasion of the Chateau Blanc masque at Greenwich Palace which took place on St Thomas's Day in December 1524. Mistress Anne wore a costume of shaded green silk with long draping sleeves and her dark auburn hair loose down her back. She danced with superlative grace and drew the eye of everyone present. I could see that the king was fascinated by her and later he would recall her appearance that evening as the Lady Greensleeves in the words of a famous song. After the masque, discreet enquiries were made regarding my availability. However, they were all refused as even then Mistress Anne would tolerate no competition from her rivals. She dressed in the French style and soon set the fashion at court for wearing the French hood. She often wore her famous pearl necklace with a gold pendant in the form of her initials. She never wore the same outfit twice, but every day she made a change in her garments. I soon became indispensable in establishing her reputation for sophistication. Sometimes she kept me sewing in her private room so that none would see her costumes until she made her entrance.

Now and again, there were summer picnics in the palace gardens where the king and queen were entertained by their courtiers. On one occasion I was summoned to bring a selection of silk threads from the sewing room. I arrived to find Sir Thomas Wyatt was reading his poetry to Mistress Anne and her needlework was laid aside. She asked him if he had written any new poems lately.

"Why yes, Mistress Anne. By your leave I will read you a couple of my verses:

Forget not yet the tried intent
Of Such a truth as I have meant;
My great travail so gladly spent,
Forget not yet.

Forget not yet when first began
The weary life ye know, since whan
The suit, the service, none tell can;
Forget not yet."

"I see it is the theme of courtly love. Will any here dare the challenge to make it a contest?"

"That will I," declared the king. "Although it is a bold challenge when Wyatt opens the lists.

As the holly grows green
And never changes hue,
So I am — ever have been —
unto my lady true.

Now unto my lady
Promise to her I make:
From all other, only
to her, I me betake.

Now, Mistress Anne. It shall be your part to play the judge between us."

"Alas, your Majesty I am no judge of such matters."

"I see you fear to speak about the love of fair ladies. But you need not shrink from it."

"Then your Majesty, I judge that the love of a faithful lady is better than the love of a forgetful one."

"So I am the winner in this game of courtly words. And I what reward do you have to give me?"

Mistress Anne smiled at him and held out her hand. "I give you this ring from my finger, your Majesty."

"I shall wear your token as a remembrance of my poem, Mistress Anne. Come, Sir Thomas, I will offer you a rematch on the bowling lawn."

In the course of the game they argued over a shot and their rivalry for Anne was revealed. Sir Thomas said that the shot was his, but King Henry insisted, "I tell you it is mine." He pointed at the bowl with the finger on which he wore Anne's ring. In response, Wyatt then drew out Anne's locket from around his neck and kissed it. King Henry was furious and broke off the game to demand an explanation from Mistress Anne. She told the king that Sir Thomas had taken her locket without her permission and that he meant nothing to her. She sent me to find Sir Thomas and demand its return. The king was appeased but Mistress Anne was most displeased.

I was embarrassed by my errand and waited until I could speak to Sir Thomas privately.

"My mistress has sent me to bring back her locket to her, Sir Thomas."

"Tell her that I will meet her in the rose garden presently," he replied.

Mistress Anne was not pleased by his answer. "Very well. But you shall accompany me there, Margery." She sat on a bench below a spray of red Tudor blossoms and pretended to embroider. I stood behind her wishing I was back at my sewing.

Soon Sir Thomas joined us and returned the locket to Mistress Anne with a bow. "I saw it dangling from your pocket while I was reading to you and could not resist drawing it out. Please say that you forgive me."

"You made a spectacle of me in front of the king, Sir Thomas. I do not deserve to be labelled as a foolish butterfly."

"I could never think of you that way. My poems express how I truly feel about you."

"And how do you feel, Sir Thomas?"

"Anne, my dearest lady. We have long been friends and neighbours. You are not just my inspiration, but the star of my heaven. I would be in your company always."

"Are you preparing another poem in my honour, Sir Thomas?"

His face fell. "It is no jest, my lady, but the deepest longing of my heart. I have wanted to speak to you ever since your coming to the court. And I can only trust to your goodness to return my regard."

Mistress Anne unfurled her fan and batted away a hovering fly. "Old friends and poets may have license to speak. But married men cannot make declarations, Sir Thomas."

"I have separated from my wife Elizabeth and intend to petition the Church for a divorce. I am asking you to be my wife, dear Anne."

"Your wife has powerful friends who will not countenance a divorce. I cannot be your wife, Sir Thomas. And my father would never allow me to become your mistress. But let us put aside such sad thoughts and continue as good friends."

"Only take courage, Anne, and entrust yourself to me. I will not fail you. We will live in my house at Allington and set the opinions of fools at naught."

"My sister Mary took that path and where has it led her? Marriage is a woman's only protection when passion has turned to dust. A true friend would care for my honour."

"I offer you my heart and hand for eternity, Anne. Will you cast them aside as if they were nothing? Will you show me no kindness after all I have said?"

"A true love is an honourable love, Sir Thomas. Would you write your poems to a defamed lady? You are not free to speak of marriage. And so I bid you farewell." Mistress Anne rose and returned to the palace leaving her would-be suitor alone in the garden. The following day he sent her another poem.

"What word is it that changeth not,
Tho' it be turned and made in twain?
It is mine Anna, God it wot,
And eke the causer of my pain,
Who love rewarded with disdain."

CHAPTER 6:
The Royal Courtship (1526)

The next year the king sent Sir Thomas Wyatt abroad on a diplomatic mission to France for he would brook no rivals in his court. The court moved to his favourite palace of Greenwich for the Shrovetide celebrations. King Henry rode out to the jousting field wearing a tabard embroidered with a burning heart and the words *Declare Je Nos* (Declare I Dare Not). It was a public announcement of his love for Mistress Anne. At the evening revels the king told her that she stood out among all the other women at court for her excellent grace and behaviour. The next day Anne wore a gold pendant which contained a set of miniature toothpicks. It was her first gift from the king.

However, Mistress Anne was unmoved by the king's attentions for she recognised that she was merely replacing her sister Mary in his affection. The next time he sent for her to press his suit she fell upon her knees saying, "I think Your Majesty, most noble and worthy king, speaks these words in mirth to prove me, without intent of defiling your princely self. I beseech Your Highness most earnestly to desist, and to take my answer in good part. I would rather lose my life than my honesty, which shall be the greatest and best part of the dowry I shall have to bring to my husband." Mistress Anne then withdrew from court and returned to Hever Castle to the great astonishment of the king, the court and her family.

One day when I came into Anne's room with her newly hemmed bed linen, she was sitting beside the window looking like the cat who had got the cream. "Tell me, Margery, did you ever have a sweetheart?"

I put down the bedlinen on the chest at the foot of the bed. "No, Mistress Anne,"

I replied stolidly. "I came here to work at the age of ten."

"Well and suppose you did have one, Margery? How would he woo you?"

"I expect that he would make me a fairing, Mistress Anne."

"You ought to prize yourself more highly than that, Margery. After all, you are now a servant of the Boleyn family."

I saw that she was had a letter in her lap and guessed that it was from a suitor. "Is there any news from court, Mistress Anne?"

"Yes, indeed," she announced grandly. "The king has sent me his greetings together with the gift of a buck which he killed in the hunt yesterday. He writes that he hopes that when I eat of it, I will think of the hunter. What do you think to that, Margery?"

I was too astounded to speak, but fortunately it was not necessary. There was a knock on the door and her mother's maid Isabel came into the room. "Your mother requests that you come to speak with her in her chamber, Mistress Anne." Anne smiled, put her letter into her sleeve and glided out. Soon the whole castle was speaking of nothing else but the fine stag which had been sent to the castle kitchen that day. This was the beginning of the king's courtship of Mistress Anne. Her mother insisted that I prepare new gowns for my mistress, so I was kept busy enough. The women servants were convinced that Mistress Anne would soon be returning to court. But this was not the case. She remained contentedly in her room at Hever reading books and composing tunes on her lute. Nobody knew what to make of it.

I become a frequent visitor to Mistress Anne's room while preparing her wardrobe. There were almost daily discussions between Lady Elizabeth and Mistress Anne about the details of each gown. Sometimes they would forget my presence in the room and speak of the king's regard for her.

"Mother, you cannot wish me to throw myself away. I desire to make a good match. The king is not free to marry and he does little for his mistresses. If I stay here at Hever he will soon forget about me and choose another. George can tell us when it is safe for me to return to the court."

"And yet we cannot afford to offend the king. He has written to you again, has he not? Have you sent him a suitable reply? It is what he expects!"

Mistress Anne produced a letter from her sleeve and handed it to her mother. "You may read it for yourself, mother."

Lady Elizabeth sat down and read it carefully, but her trembling hands showed her agitation. "Why he says that he has been struck with the dart of love above a whole year!"

"I can scarcely believe it mother, since my sister Mary's child was only born this March. It is no pleasure to me to receive the king's attentions before the eyes of the queen. I would rather have an honest courtship and an honourable marriage."

"But look, he writes that he wishes to take you as his only mistress. You would be his maitress-en-titre and receive due respect."

"He asks me to give myself up body and heart to him which he has no right to do. He asks me to become his mistress but offers nothing in return. It is an insult. He deserves no answer."

"Take care, my child. You cannot scorn the king. He is a most vengeful man and all at court know it."

"Do we want to be known as the family which gave up both their daughters to the king's lust? We will become the laughing-stock of the nobility."

"I am only saying to act with care. He can make us or ruin us as you well know."

"Then I shall send him the only answer that is proper to make. I will tell him plainly that his wife I cannot be, both in respect of mine own unworthiness, and because he has a queen already. And his mistress I will not be. That will put an end to the matter."

But surprising to say, it did not. If anything, it seemed to redouble the king's ardour. He sent her a present of a gold brooch in the form of a lady holding a crown to tell the story of his love. In this way, the king offered Mistress Anne the place of queen rather than that of his mistress. The family took counsel together and decided that the state of honourable marriage should not be refused. Sir Thomas Boleyn commissioned a costly jewel in the form of a storm-tossed damsel in a ship of safety. And Mistress Anne composed a courtly love letter to the king reciprocating his great love towards her and her desire to submit herself entirely to his protection.

The king speedily expressed his thanks for her beautiful gift and its tender meaning. He was filled with delight that she returned his love and promised to honour, love and serve her alone. He hoped that the time would be short until he saw her again. That letter was soon followed by another in which he enclosed his likeness set in a bracelet as a reminder of his love saying that he wished himself in its place. To this Mistress Anne sent a reply, thanking him for his generous favour in appointing her as maid of honour to the queen and looking forward to seeing him at court.

On her return to court Mistress Anne was graciously received by Queen Catherine. The king selected Mistress Anne as his partner before the entire court and the French ambassadors at Greenwich. I witnessed the courtship of King Henry and Mistress Anne and recorded it in a procession of dresses, each one finer than the last, for her sent her bolts of the finest silks and satins in the kingdom. There were lengths of cloth of gold, purple satin and crimson velvet for new gowns. These colours were the very badge of royalty and it was regarded as presumptuous for mere nobles to wear them, but no-one dared to say about it. Anne was now at liberty to wear whatever she desired. Arnold the court shoemaker received quantities of black velvet to make shoes and slippers for her. And the king ordered costly jewels from his goldsmith Cornelius Hayes, including nineteen diamonds set in trueloves of gold to adorn her head. Mistress Anne was now the queen in all but name. It was said that she was the model and the mirror of those who were at court, for she was unrivalled in the gracefulness of her attire, and every day made some change in the fashion of her garments. And if ever a man loved a woman, I can attest that King Henry so loved the lady Anne. He declared that he loved her so much that he would beg alms from door to door rather than give her up. Indeed, the king and Mistress Anne even exchanged love notes as they sat together in the royal chapel. She wrote a message to him in a prayer book which read, "By daily proof you shall me find, to be to you both loving and kind."

The king kept his promise and raised her from a commoner to a queen of England. When she first arrived in court from France I believe that no man could have resisted her. She outshone all the other ladies by her wit, her charm and her learning. She dressed in the French style and drew the eye like a poppy in a field of wheat. She excelled at the game of courtship and indeed the king spent seven years in pursuit of her. He swore that he would tear down the world to make her his lawful wife, and truly he did.

CHAPTER 7:

THE KING'S GREAT MATTER (1527)

Naturally, the situation created tensions for the courtiers hardly knew whether to acknowledge Queen Catherine or Mistress Anne. One day when Queen Catherine was playing cards with Mistress Anne, she said: "Lady Anne, you have the good fortune to always stop at a king. But you are not like the others, you will have all, or none." Mistress Anne was displeased to discover that Queen Catherine was still sewing the king's shirts and said that she wished that all Spaniards were at the bottom of the sea. When Queen Catherine proposed to the king that the Princess Mary should pay them a visit he replied that she could go to Ludlow if she wanted to visit and stay there. But the queen replied that she would never leave him for her proper place was at his side.

Rumours began to spread through the court regarding the King's Great Matter. At first it was whispered that Queen Catherine would retire from the life of court into a nunnery. But she made it clear that she would have none of it, insisting "God never called me to a nunnery. I am the king's true and legitimate wife." It was then said that the king would seek an annulment. In May 1529 Queen Catherine appeared before the Legatine Court at Blackfriars and appealed to the king for justice saying, "These twenty years and more I have been your true wife. And when you had me at the first, I take God to be my judge I was true maid without touch of man." The court adjourned without a verdict and its failure marked the downfall of Cardinal Wolsey. Pope Clement ordered the king to separate from Mistress Anne and take back Queen Catherine as his wife. He was forbidden to remarry under penalty of excommunication. If he did, then his children would not be legitimate.

Mistress Anne reproached the king with the waste of her time and youth when she might have contracted an advantageous marriage. She had read a new book by William Tyndale called "The Obedience of the Christian Man" and gave it to the king. King Henry was impressed by its argument that kings were only accountable to God. He pronounced it a book "for me and all kings to read." Finally, Archbishop Thomas Cranmer declared King Henry's marriage null and void claiming that it was contrary to divine law since Queen Catherine had previously been married to his brother.

King Henry tried his best to placate Mistress Anne throughout these difficulties. She was given her own lodgings at Hampton Court and sat beside the king at banquets wearing gowns of purple to mark her pre-eminence. Her father and brother were both granted earldoms. And when he went on his summer progress in 1529 he took Mistress Anne with him and told Queen Catherine to leave before he returned. She was given the palace of The More as her residence. Mistress Anne pointed out that she still had a staff of over two hundred servants which was quite ridiculous in her view. "The old woman should have gone into a convent. Preferably one in Spain." She insisted that Queen Catherine should return all the jewels that rightfully belonged to the queen of England. And the king sent the Duke of Norfolk to reclaim them. They were reset into fine new pieces for Mistress Anne. Only the Spanish Ambassador Chapuys was bold enough to reproach Henry for his treatment of Queen Catherine. But the king was not abashed. "God and his conscience were perfectly agreed on that point," he said. He wished to secure the succession of his kingdom by having children which he had not at present.

I can recall the happiness of those first years at court before the king's regard for Mistress Anne turned to dark suspicion. Henry was determined that his court would out-rival those of France and Spain to be the greatest in Christendom. He built great palaces and gardens without concern for the cost. Thomas More described the royal court as *"a temple of the muses"* for it included the illustrious painters Han Holbein and Lucas Horenbout, the composers William Byrd and Thomas Tallis and the poets Thomas Wyatt and Thomas Seymour. Henry and Anne could both sing, play the lute and compose their own songs. One of Henry's favourites was *"My Lute Awake"* which he would sing to the lady Anne. He would often challenge their courtiers to contests of poetry and music which inspired wonderful nights of entertainment in the tradition of courtly love.

CHAPTER 8:

The Court Musician (1530)

It was on one of these nights that I first crossed paths with Mark Smeaton. He was a Flemish lute-player who was attracted to the Tudor court by its reputation for generous patronage. And a notably handsome young man who could sing, dance and play several instruments. The music for that evening took the form of "The Battle of the Lutes" and was a great success. As a concession I was permitted to remain and listen to the players competing. Mark was judged to be the winner of the contest and rewarded with a purse of gold. Then the company withdrew to attend the banquet leaving us both alone in the hall. Mark was still flushed with his triumph and looking to share it with an audience, even one as poor as I.

"What is your name, mistress?"

"It is Margery Hallows."

"It suits you."

I wrinkled my nose. "I don't care for it."

"Why not?"

"When I was a child my brothers would tease me by singing "See-saw, Margery Daw" over and over again."

"Who is Margery Daw?"

"It's just an old children's rhyme."

Of course, he had never heard of it being from Flanders. That night he sang me some of the folksongs of his homeland. It is a night that I will always cherish for he sang for me alone. And so our friendship began. Afterwards, Mistress Anne often sent for him to play for the company. This is how I came to know him for she would also send for me to discuss her choice of robes. Later, we would be dismissed and we would talk together discreetly. It soon became a habit and we became trusted friends.

"What brought you to England instead of the French court, Mark?"

"The French court has many accomplished musicians and the courtiers are very well connected. Often you have to pay a patron to find you a place in the court. Here there is less competition and you can make your own way if you have the talent. I began as a boy singer in the choir of Cardinal Wolsey. After he fell from favour I joined the Chapel Royal. I came to the attention of the king because I was not only a fine singer, but I could play many instruments well. Not only the lute, but the viol, the virginals and the organ. And I could dance as well as any courtier."

"How do you like it here at court?"

"It is the best place for a musician to make his fortune. It was here at court that I first met Mistress Anne. She sent for me to play the virginals while Sir Henry Norris was leading her out to dance and she said to him, "What do you think of it, does not the lad play well?" Then she told me that I would be one of musicians of the royal household and gave me a hundred nobles to buy new clothes. It marked the start of my court career for she persuaded the king to give me a salary of £100 to support my position. As you know, Mistress Hallows, it is the way you dress at court that makes all the difference. I admire Mistress Anne because she has brought the French style to the English court. If you did not know, you would take her for a born Frenchwoman."

I had noticed that Mark was far better dressed than the other musicians and looked as fine as the son of a gentleman. I was amazed at how highly prized were the musicians, for as a seamstress at the court I earned only twenty pounds. It was true that the king liked to surround himself with handsome men and woman and gave abundant gifts to his favourites. "Were your parents musicians too?"

He shook his head. "Not they. My father was a carpenter and my mother was a seamstress like you, Mistress Hallows. She also made lace for the gentry. So I always wore good clothes. And as a singer I was provided with choir dress. But the dress of a courtier has a language of its own. If you are fashionable and elegant then you will be noticed even if you are of mean birth. The king is a generous patron of music and he recognises my abilities. I have hopes that he will entrust me to organise some of the court entertainments."

"I would like to learn the skill of making lace," I said. "But I have no time to spare. I am so busy every day and often I work late into the night."

"You will find it is worthwhile to develop your gifts, Mistress Hallows. Even if you have to pay to learn the skill from another. Perhaps when the king goes on his summer progress you will have time."

I shook my head. "Mistress Anne always takes me with her. Sometimes we go to visit Hever, but there are no lacemakers there."

"You have to seek out the opportunities," he emphasised. "You cannot wait for them to come to you." I realised that this was Mark's philosophy. He had a plan for his future whereas I had not thought beyond a life in service to the Boleyn family. Perhaps he was right and I should learn some new skills. But when I spoke to Lady Lee she would not hear of it. "Mistress Anne requires your full attention to attend the needs of her wardrobe. As a court dressmaker you have all the scope you need to become a notable seamstress. There are others who excel at lacemaking, blackwork embroidery and silk making. But there is no need for you to spend your time on them. There will always be plenty of work available for a skilled dressmaker." Fortunately, this proved to be true. But I regret that I never had a chance to learn lacemaking for it was a good way for a woman to earn herself a living.

One day Mistress Anne sent for me to come to her apartments and showed me four French saddles of black velvet with gold and silk fringes. "These are a gift from the king," she said with a satisfied air. "He wishes me to share his pleasures when he goes out riding. You are to make me a riding outfit to match. It shall be black velvet with a gold trim. And loose enough in the skirt to enable me to ride pillion behind the king."

"Yes, Mistress Anne," I said feeling somewhat bewildered as I had never made a riding costume before.

She frowned slightly. "It is not so different from a dance costume, Margery. The bodice should be tight fitting but the skirts should be full. The king has also given me a set of gloves and Arnold is making me a pair of black leather boots to wear. You must both be ready in two days' time."

"Yes, Mistress Anne," I repeated and curtsied as I left. The next two days were an anxious time. Lady Lee recommended that I sewed small lead weights into the hem of the skirt so that it would fall easily into place. I brought it to Mistress Anne to try on and she pronounced herself satisfied.

"I must select the jewels for the bodice and the velvet bonnet," she said. "The king likes to ride out at dawn so all must be ready."

But it was not until the afternoon that the king was free to go out riding. That evening Mark came to seek me out. He had been included in the party to entertain the king and Mistress Anne with songs and music. "I tell you, Margery, you should have been there." My heart skipped a beat. Had he missed me then? But no, his attention was not on me but on his inner thoughts. He had only sought me out as a sympathetic listener so that he could relive his glorious day. "This is what it means to really live," he declared with a radiant face. "We rode out to a pavilion in the forest. The cooks were already waiting with the banquet. They feasted and afterwards I played for them. The king and Mistress Anne requested their favourite love songs and drank toasts to each other."

I suspected that he had been handsomely rewarded, but he didn't mention it. He was too caught up in the atmosphere of the day. "What did they ask you play for them?"

"I will tell you the whole of it. I played and sang for the best part of the afternoon. They complimented me as the perfect herald of love and then Mistress Anne borrowed my lute to play for the king herself. She played most beautifully and the king was enchanted. Then the king took the lute and sang his own song Greensleeves to her. He said that so he had seen her on the night of the Chateau Blanc masque and knew her for his lady. Mistress Anne kissed his hand and swore that a thousand deaths would not part her from him. The king was deeply moved and desired us to withdraw and leave them. I shall play you all the songs that I performed for them, Margery, "As the holly growth green," "Complain I may," "Fair and discreet" and "My woeful heart." And so he played - and played wonderfully - but his thoughts were not of me, but of his lady, the unattainable and distainful Greensleeves.

"Alas, my love, that you should own
A heart of wanton vanity,
So must I meditate alone
Upon your insincerity?

Well, I will pray to God on high,
That thou my constancy mayst see,
And that yet once before I die,
Thou wilt vouchsafe to love me."

Evidently, the riding habit was a success, for I received an order to make exact copies in dark blue, emerald green and violet velvet. It was such a considerable task that it required the combined skills of the sewing room for a week. Mary Dacre muttered that she knew why Mistress Anne liked to ride out with the king for then she could have him all to herself. It was true. Mark had confided to me that the riding trips were more enjoyable than entertaining in the court for there were no quarrelsome courtiers or haughty nobles to spoil the pleasure. It meant that the king and Mistress Anne could escape from the oppressive gossip of the court and the reports of the foreign ambassadors.

When New Year came I gave Mark a fine kerchief embroidered with a design of his initials each side of a lute. He told me it was the finest thing he owned and he would always treasure it. He was always gallant that way. That evening after the revels I told Mark how much I wished that I had learned to dance.

"If it were known that you could not dance then you would be sent home tomorrow in disgrace," he said humorously. "Surely you have watched the ladies of the court dancing many times?"

"I have seen them, but I have never dared to try it for myself," I confessed.

"Then it will be my honour to teach you, Mistress Hallows. We will begin with a pavane. I will hum the tune as we practice the steps."

He was a highly accomplished dancer and delighted to share his skills even with a complete beginner. He told me which ladies to watch and who were the best exponents of each form. I realised that he had made a complete study of the skills of the court.

"You have not mentioned Mistress Anne," I observed.

"It is not my place to comment on her," he replied proudly. "But she is superlative as she is in everything. Her style is incomparable and she is not afraid to improvise. What a partner she would make! How much I regret my low degree whenever I see her favouring one of these lumpish courtiers. None of them are worthy of her! But of course, you will not repeat what I have said!"

"Of course I will not, Mark," I assured him. "But you must not speak of this to anyone else."

"I must say them to someone for they are eating out my heart. How hard it is to find the perfect counterpart in the dance, but we will never combine our skills together. Just once I long to do so, but it can never be!"

"You will overthrow the court, Mark. It would be like King Henry coming to practice sewing with me."

"You make a joke of it, but I am in earnest! Goodnight, Mistress Hallows."

Afterwards I regretted that I had not given him better counsel, for he never spoke of her again. A true friend would have advised him to find a partner in his own degree. But how could I say so, when that was my own dearest wish? I had heard the story of Charles Brandon, Duke of Suffolk, who had married the king's sister Mary without his permission. He was of noble birth and a close friend of King Henry, but it still almost cost him his life. I wondered if Mark also knew this story or if his feelings made him reckless. For my part, I found it safer never to say much in the presence of my betters. But then, I was no courtier to risk my place in the hope of preferment. My humble background instilled in me the caution to value what I had more than vain dreams and ambitions.

We were both talented but lowly born and so the court was at once a delight and a torment for we could never hope to take an equal place there. One night as we battled it out on the chessboard Mark argued that the times were changing and that the king's advisers Wolsey, More and Cromwell had risen from relative obscurity to high rank by their abilities.

"They were lawyers," I pointed out. "You are a musician and I am a dressmaker. We may gain favour but we will always be servants. We can never rise to a place in the court."

"I may be a servant, but I still have the heart of a gentleman."

"We are not just servants, Mark. We are royal servants. It will be something for us to tell our grandchildren one day."

"It is true. We were chosen out of many for royal service. Our talents have brought us this far and may take us further still, if we have hope and courage. I am a rising figure in the court. I began as a chorister to Cardinal Wolsey, but I am now a court musician to the king himself. He has rewarded me with rich purses and Mistress Anne has favoured me too. And I am still young and have time on my side."

I did not have the heart to topple his castles in the air. I thought that as a foreigner Mark had simply failed to understand the limitations of English society. The nobility would not tolerate ambitious commoners, no matter how able they were. It was true that Cardinal Wolsey had been the son of a butcher but lived like a prince and had built himself two great palaces in London. But the nobility bitterly resented his success and had never let him forget his origins. Later, I came to realise that Mark had fallen desperately in love with Mistress Anne and could not accept that there was no hope for him. I wish that I had warned him, but by then I was deeply in love myself. I lived for the brief moments when we could meet together and he lived for the rare times when Mistress Anne would deign to notice him.

CHAPTER 9:

"The Most Happy" (1532-1533)

After Queen Catherine was sent from the court and re-titled as the Princess Dowager, the fortunes of Mistress Anne continued to rise. The first momentus event was her elevation to the rank of Marquis of Pembroke in September 1532. For once, I was one of the first to hear the news for it was my task to create a magnificent costume for the occasion. Mistress Anne sent for me to come to her chamber where a great bolt of crimson velvet had just been delivered for her approval.

"You shall make me a velvet gown trimmed with ermine fur, Margery. And a mantle to match it. It must be your best work, you understand? There can be no mistakes!"

"Yes, Mistress Anne. It will be the finest that has ever been seen," I assured her. It was the only acceptable response.

"After the ceremony you will refer to me as Lady Anne," she informed me. And it was a great occasion indeed. Mistress Anne was brought before the king at Windsor Castle in the presence of the greatest nobles in the land. He placed upon her the mantle and coronet and gave her the patent of nobility. She was also granted lands worth £1000 a year to maintain her in the dignity of her new position.

Mistress Anne was not a particularly considerate mistress for she was far too self-centred to consider the feelings of others. But I knew she was pleased with her splendid costume for afterward she arranged for my introduction to King Henry.

"So you are the girl with the marvellous fingers," he declared, beaming at me. Faced with the full onslaught of the royal Tudor charm I fell into stammers. But it didn't displease him. As much as he admired the witty repartee of his courtiers, he was still more flattered to know that his mere presence could strike his subjects dumb.

"Lady Anne has told me of your devotion. We were pleased with the robes you made for the ceremony. So we are pleased to give you this token of our regard." He handed me a small bag of black velvet. Inside was a fine silver thimble embellished with his initials HR.

"Thank you, your Majesty," I managed to say and made my best curtsey.

"You will be the envy of the sewing room," remarked Lady Anne complacently as if envy was a desirable achievement.

"How do you like it here at court, Mistress Hallows?"

I pulled myself together. "I think it is the most wonderful place in the world. It is a great honour to serve here, your Majesty."

"Well said," he replied kindly. But his attention was already returning to Lady Anne. "We must make sure that your mistress has a setting that is truly worthy of her. And that reminds me. We have to decide the music for this evening. Shall we have the singers or the recorders?

"Let us have both," she decided. "And let them bring something new for us this time." Then she gave me a little push. "Off with you now, girl. Back to your sewing." I curtseyed to them both and backed carefully out of the room. Arousing the jealousy of my fellow-servants was the last thing I wanted to do, so I decided not to wear it. Instead, I put the king's gift away carefully in my bundle.

But the next time I was called to Lady Anne's apartments to make an alteration she noticed its absence and was displeased. "Why are you using that old thing? Why aren't you wearing the king's thimble? It is an honour!"

"I was afraid of losing it, Lady Anne," I replied. "I wish to keep it as an heirloom."

"Nonsense," she snapped. "The king will expect to see you wearing it. Go and put it on!"

And so whenever I was called to sew in public I took care to wear the royal thimble. As I feared, it led to cold looks in the sewing room and cutting remarks about favouritism. It is true that all the seamstresses worked hard and it was unfair only to reward the ones who do the most elaborate work. But life at court was often unfair and certain members of the court gained far more rewards than others. I could see that Mark was beginning to brood on the fact that despite having superior talents to most of the courtiers, he was still held back by his lack of noble birth. There was an invisible barrier beyond which he could not step. "I am no more than one of their pet spaniels – to be petted and then dismissed as they please," he grumbled. "Look at Master Holbein. He has made his fortune as the king's favourite artist. And yet his birth is no better than mine! I am young, handsome and talented. Why cannot I make my way?"

"Why can't I have what I want?" I mentally translated. But even the king could not always get what he wanted. The sons and daughters of the poor were fortunate to find employment when so many laboured in the fields. I knew that Mark lived much better than most household musicians and far better than his own family in Flanders. But he could no longer appreciate how far he had come in life. He was frustrated that he could not share the privileges of the nobility as an equal. He could not presume to match with them in their games of wit, nor compete with them at cards nor court the lady of his choice. I was sorry to see that his courtier's life was becoming more of a source of discontent than a pleasure to him. He was of a different spirit from myself. He shared the sensual vitality and quick wits of the Queen. And just like her, he yearned to be the centre of admiration. He wasn't content to be an admirer.

For my part, I could clearly see the advantages which I enjoyed as a court seamstress – my salary, food, board and clothing – compared to the endless toil of the wife of a farmer. It was far beyond my father's hopes for me. Those who lived at court need not live in fear of the weather and the harvest. I realised that I was more content at court than Mark because I didn't covet attention and recognition. The Queen had become possessive over my services and that was my best security. Even her mother no longer had her gowns made by me. And when a favourite young lady in waiting had asked if I could make a pair of embroidered sleeves for her, the Queen had betrayed her annoyance. "Mistress Hallows has quite enough to do already." No-one ever asked again for they could see that she regarded me as her exclusive property.

A more worldly servant than I might have taken the opportunity to seek a higher salary. Indeed, my father had bartered my services at Hever for the highest price for he knew what was due to him. As the youngest in a motherless family I had found consolation in my craft. And as a royal servant I took care never to outshine my mistress for I sensed that she would endure no rivals. She might call me a mouse and a sparrow and sneer at my lack of sophistication, but that was better than arousing her hostility. My quiet ways spared me from becoming the focus of her temper. And my humility was my protection among the other servants. If I had conducted myself arrogantly as the best seamstress at court, I might have become the victim of envy. But since I had the favour of Queen Anne no-one troubled me. On the one occasion when Mary Dacre had made mischief by hiding my threads and moving my pins she had been roundly scolded by Lady Lee for damaging the Queen's prestige. "Pride goes before a fall," Mistress Carew had always said. How true that was of the court where a newcomer might be a novelty one day, but fall out of favour the next. What was the secret to success at court I wondered? Clearly, it was to gain lasting royal favour. But favour was elusive and no-one was indispensible. There were always more courtiers in waiting.

In October 1532 it was announced that King Henry and Lady Anne were going to travel to Calais to meet King Francis I. For King Henry wanted the Lady Anne to be recognised by the royal houses of Europe. Immediately, the order came down to the sewing room for a gown of cloth of gold spangled with diamonds and a sash of crimson satin for her meeting with the French king. When it was completed, I looked forward to a rest from my labours. But Lady Anne insisted that I should accompany her to Calais in case she needed my skills. I was most unwilling to journey so far to an unknown land where I could not speak a word of the language. However, Lady Anne was entirely unsympathetic to my fears. "Why Margery, I travelled to France as a child of only seven. Tis true, that travelling by sea can be unpleasant. But this is an opportunity for you to see the French court. I want you to keep your eyes open and mark the latest ladies' fashions so that we can take them back to England." And so I was present when Lady Anne made her entrance after the royal banquet splendidly apparelled in her royal cloth of gold. She danced adroitly with the French king and then sat down with him in private conversation. This meant that her position was acknowledged by the French court.

After our return from France, the Lady Anne was in high spirits. She sent for me on numerous occasions to discuss what we had both seen of the fashions of the French court and to plan several new gowns to be made in the latest French style. I remember that for the first of these designs I was called to her apartments to prepare a jewelled setting for the square neckline of her bodice. It was then that I noticed her jewel box which was the size of a small chest and stood upon a sturdy trestle table. It contained a vast selection of earrings, necklaces, bracelets and brooches. There were ropes of matched pearls, rubies set in gold roses and diamonds set in lovers' knots. And there were jewelled billaments for hoods and embossed gold lozenges set with rubies, pearls and diamonds to embellish gowns. These were all provided by the king to demonstrate her station at court. The Lady Anne noticed my amazement and smiled slightly. She was invariably in a good humour when ordering a new costume for it was one of her favourite pursuits. "This will be a new gown of tawny velvet with gold satin sleeves for Christmastide. You are to make a triple border along the neckline, Margery. The top row will be of pearls, the second row of spaced square-cut rubies and the bottom row worked of gold thread embroidery. The goldsmith will make gold settings for each of the jewels so that you may sew them securely onto the gown. You must do the work here in my apartments so that none of the gems are lost or damaged." I was astonished by the sight of such costly jewels to be used for the edging of a dress. But this regal extravagance soon became the typical style of the Lady Anne's costumes for the king gave her numerous gifts of jewels and she was determined to outshine the French royal fashions at the English court.

Sewing in the queen's apartments made a pleasant change from the sewing room. The ladies in waiting were always eager to have a sight of the queen's latest costumes, but she would always shoo them away to maintain the surprise. I could hear the musicians as they played and sang for the queen and her ladies. Mark was frequently present in their company and he nicknamed me Mistress Nimblefingers to the great amusement of all. Sometimes the king would visit and I would hear him conversing with the queen or playing at cards with her ladies. At other times, eminent visitors would come to pay their respects which never failed to please her. On Sundays, the queen's chaplains would come to preach sermons or read devout books and they would frown to see me industriously plying my needle as they passed by my table. However,

Queen Anne would allow no-one to interfere with the making of her gowns and none of them were bold enough to rebuke her vanity.

The Christmas festivities in Greenwich that year were especially joyous for the old queen was now residing at Enfield and so the court was undivided in its attentions to the Lady Anne. It was only too clear that her star was on the rise and the king could not do enough for her. She lived like a queen and presided over all the court festivities during the twelve nights. It was said that she had bewitched the king for he accompanied her to Mass and everywhere she went. It seemed like a dream that a young girl from a modest estate in Kent should rise to become the highest in the land. One freezing night in the Great Hall the servers came around with trays of hot ale and hot spiced wine and the courtiers were invited to toast the Lord of Misrule every time he led out one of the gentlemen to entertain the company with a festive song. The dancers and musicians were glad of an opportunity to rest from their exertions and so I found myself standing among the watchers with Mark. His eyes were gleaming with pleasure for there was nothing he enjoyed more than an evening of celebration.

"Our master and mistress are making merry together this Christmas," I remarked as I warmed my fingers against the tankard.

"And we are their merrymakers," he replied. "Without us how could they look so fine or impress their foreign guests so well? The ambassadors are bound to say that this is the finest court in Europe."

"The Lady Anne is the very picture of a queen, is she not?"

"And very much in the French style of fashion."

"They brought back quantities of the finest fabrics from the mercers of Calais so now she can indulge her every fancy. The king is only pleased if he can please her."

"Then she has already gained heaven on earth. That is what is means to captivate a king."

"She believes that she is the new Esther whom the king raised up to be his queen."

"Indeed, she has risen far. And her faithful servants will rise with her. The king has just appointed me as a Groom of the Privy Court. It is a great mark of favour, and it shows he makes no distinctions among his servants but rewards the men of talent as much as the men of birth." He was delighted with his life at court that Christmastide and had high hopes for his future.

At New Year the customary presentation of gifts was made. King Henry gave Lady Anne hangings of cloth of gold, cloth of silver and embroidered crimson satin for her room and bed. And in return she gave him a set of richly decorated boar spears. It was whispered that the exiled queen Catherine had sent the king a gold cup, but he had refused to accept it and sent it back to her. Many other valuable gifts were presented to the king including a silver-gilt compass, a clock and a marmoset and he in his turn gave gifts to the court and royal servants. Mark received a cambric shirt and a shaving cloth and all the seamstresses were given fine ivory combs for dressing our hair. That Christmas marked the height of happiness at the court for King Henry and the Lady Anne had now achieved their heart's desire after seven years of waiting.

And then, I was admitted to news of a great secret. The Lady Anne was expecting the king's child. I must be ready to adapt all her dresses to fit her in the months to come. Lady Lee was also informed as she would have to supply the extra lengths of fabric from her store. This happy news prompted the marriage of King Henry and the Lady Anne to take place immediately, for the king would have a legitimate heir. In January 1533 they were married in a secret ceremony in the Chapel Royal. The king took Lady Anne to visit the Jewel House and she wore the finest of the Crown Jewels on the day. I made the wedding dress for the occasion from white satin and tissue of silver. However, there are no secrets in a royal court and there was open speculation among the courtiers and ambassadors that the king had remarried.

The conjecture in the court was laid to rest at Easter 1533 when the Lady Anne made her first public appearance as the queen dressed in a gown of gold silk spangled with diamonds and pearls. She was attended by sixty maids of honour. The foreign ambassadors reported that it looked like a dream and even her own supporters did not know whether to laugh or to cry. Her royal household was formed of two hundred and fifty servants. She appointed Lord Burgh as her chamberlain, her uncle Sir James Boleyn as her chancellor, William Coffin as Master of the Horse, John Skip as her almoner and Hugh Latimer, William Betts and Matthew Parker as her household chaplains.

The king made plans for an elaborate coronation ceremony in London. On 29th May Lady Anne was escorted to the Tower by river. On 30th May eighteen Knights of the Bath were created. On 31st May the Lady Anne processed into London carried in a litter all dressed in white with a coronet of gold. However, the splendid display was not enough for her to win the favour of the crowds. The king later asked her, "How liked you the look of the city?" And she replied, "Sir, I liked the city well enough, but I saw a great many caps on heads and heard but few tongues"' One of the courtiers whispered that the people standing along the route looked as sorry as though it had been a funeral. On 1st June she was crowned as queen by Archbishop Cranmer at a solemn mass in Westminster Abbey. She wore coronation robes of purple velvet trimmed with ermine and walked under a canopy of cloth of gold. Afterwards she celebrated the occasion with a coronation banquet in Westminster Hall. The first course consisted of twenty-eight dishes and the second course twenty-three dishes. The subtleties at the end of the feast included gilded marchpane in the shape of falcons, swans and castles.

The lady Anne saw herself as the heroine of her own story – the first commoner to be crowned as queen. "What about Elizabeth Woodstock?" her detractors muttered among themselves. She took as her device a white falcon, the symbol of purity and I learned to embroider it so finely that it was as clear as a painted miniature. There was envy in the sewing room when Mistress Harvey held it up as the standard to which they should all aspire. My mistress said nothing to me, for she did not like to admit that a servant could be her superior in any of the feminine arts. But Mistress Harvey told me privately that she had once said that had I been a boy I would have made a worthy apprentice to Master Holbein. It was the greatest compliment I ever received.

CHAPTER 10:

The Falcon's Descent (1534)

On 7th September 1533 the Princess Elizabeth was born at the Palace of Greenwich. The king put a good face on the matter saying that they were both young and by God's grace boys would follow. Queen Anne sewed the robe for her christening with her own hands. And on 10th September she was given a magnificent service at the Church of the Observant Friars. But as the king it was his duty to have a son and heir. He had married his brother's widow Catherine when he was eighteen and she was twenty-six. She was too old for him and unable to bear a living son. And without a male heir the nation would have been plunged back into the tumult of the civil wars again. A divorce was a necessity. But neither Queen Catherine nor Pope Clement would concede it. And Anne was proud and ambitious, over-conscious of her Howard blood. She would not be a mistress, only a wife. And she promised him sons. But after waiting seven years for a divorce, she gave him a daughter. And the following year she suffered a miscarriage. By then her demands and tantrums no longer enchanted him. He told her that she had good reason to be content with what he had done for her and to consider from what she had come. It was not enough for her to be the queen and she lacked the royal dignity of Queen Catherine. Her temper had turned shrewish.

Although I was a simple unlettered woman, I came to understand that King Henry and Queen Anne saw themselves as figures in a great romance. All the court pageants followed that same theme. But in real life, endless romantic love was difficult to sustain. Living at such close quarters I could not help but see that King Henry was highly conceited and Anne was over-demanding. They were both strong personalities who expected constant adulation from their retinue. The servants whispered that the old queen Catherine of Aragon had been gracious and considerate to all in the manner of true royalty. King Henry had not appreciated her and Queen Anne simply could not compare. Even the king was said to have complained to the Duke of Norfolk that she was not like the old queen who had never in her life used ill words to him.

One day when I came to sew in Lady Anne's apartments, I found that she was deeply angered. Her mother Lady Elizabeth was deep in conversation with her, and I gathered that her widowed sister Mary had secretly remarried a soldier in the garrison at Calais named William Stafford. And she was already expecting a child.

"How dare she do this, mother? I would have found her a far better match if only she had waited. The very least of my ladies in waiting would not have thrown themselves away in such a manner. Has she no loyalty to me as her sister and her queen?"

"It was very wrong of her, your Majesty, not to consult with her parents or yourself. But she is still one of the family."

"Not to me, mother. I will not see her. She is forbidden to come to court. I will not share in her humiliation and disgrace. She has made her choice. So now let her live with it!"

"Yes, you are quite right, your Majesty. She is no longer a Boleyn but a Stafford. So they will have to support her in the future."

"Mother, you can't know what a terrible burden it is to be the queen. There are times when I feel utterly lonely and I can feel the eyes of the entire whole English court spying on me. If I can't count upon my own family to support me and uphold my dignity, then how can I hope to withstand my rivals? They circle me like wolves and I know that they are just biding their time for me to make a mistake."

"You are not alone, my child. Your uncle is the Duke of Norfolk, the highest peer in the land. As long as he is at your side then no-one can threaten you."

The pressure of life at the royal court affected us all. One day a drama broke out in the sewing room. The ever-vigilant Lady Lee discovered a seamstress called Nan Cobham secreting a piece of fine cambric inside her bodice. She confessed that she intended to give it as a present to a pageboy she admired. Inevitably, she was dismissed at once and the pageboy sternly warned. He protested that he had never encouraged her to give him presents so nothing could be proved against him. But Mary Dacre whispered to us that he was the guilty party. He had demanded a token and she was foolish enough to oblige him. "It's always the case that the woman is blamed. Now she has lost her place and all for nothing." Naturally, we were all given a tremendous lecture on keeping the Commandments. "The queen has said that she would be honestly served," said Lady Lee.

Sometimes I thought back enviously to the peaceful life of the farm. Often my eyes burned and my fingers ached as I rushed to alter yet another seam at the last minute.

"Why wasn't it right the first time?" Queen Anne would storm at me. "I shall tell the king this delay is your fault!"

Lady Lee often looked harried and the seamstresses whispered their complaints at every opportunity. Mary Dacre, who was bolder than the rest of us, left a pin in a seam which caused outrage. Queen Anne demanded that the royal chaplain preach a sermon series on the duty of service for the improvement of our morals. One day she flew into a royal temper over the discontented mutterings of her servants.

"Enough of your grumbling. Have done! The perfect servant never tires, never grumbles and is always ready to serve. In fact, they should perform their duties before I ask and without my knowing they are there." To impress the lesson she had me embroider the words "Aisi sera groigne qui groigne" (Let them grumble; that is how it is going to be) on the livery coats of all her servants.

King Henry smirked when he saw it. "Yes, gossip is the bane of court life. We masters bear it as our cross."

"Well, I'm not going to bear it any more," she snapped. "The next grumbler I hear will be sent home bag and baggage."

Naturally this caused resentment. It was about this time that her favourite dog Perkoy mysteriously fell out of a window to his death. Queen Anne was inconsolable and refused to hear of a new puppy. However, the king was wiser in mitigating the dissatisfaction. One day when the queen had gone out to play a game of archery he made a tour of her apartments and commended the servants for their good service. We seamstresses received a box of sweetmeats to share although he knew that the queen disapproved of servants eating from their master's table. It made us spoiled and lazy, she said. However, the king understood human nature better and the discontent settled down.

CHAPTER 11:
THUNDER ROLLS AROUND THE THRONE (1536)

The tragedy unfolded when it was least expected. In January 1536 the old queen, Catherine of Aragon, died at Kimbolton Castle. "Now I am indeed a queen!" said Anne. She and Henry dressed in yellow and celebrated together, but he came to realise that now he was free to divorce and marry again if he chose. On the very day of the former queen's funeral came the disaster of another miscarriage. Henry declared, "You will get no more sons from me." And Queen Anne protested, "You should be more bound to me than any man can be to a woman." The king became embittered towards Queen Anne. There were no more gifts – at least not for her. Other ladies of the court were singled out for attention instead. His eye fell upon Jane Seymour whom he had met on a visit to her family home at Wulf Hall the previous summer. In April1536 he sent her a purse of sovereigns accompanied by a letter as a sign of his favour. In response, Jane respectfully kissed the letter, returned it to the messenger without opening it, and then falling on her knees, begged the royal messenger to entreat the king in her name to consider that she was a well-born damsel, the daughter of good and honourable parents without blame or reproach of any kind; there was no treasure in this world that she valued as much as her honour, and on no account would she lose it And if the king wished to make her a present of money, she requested him to reserve it for such a time as God would be pleased to send her some advantageous marriage. As a result of this virtuous refusal the king's love for Jane had increased marvellously.

The Seymour family were quick to take advantage of the king's favour. Under their guidance Jane began setting the fashion for English dress in the court wearing gable hoods edged with pearls and a girdle of pearls. Her female relatives and friends all followed suit. Soon there was a visible rivalry manifesting itself in costume between the supporters of the queen and the Seymour faction. This galvanised Queen Anne's competitive spirit and she was determined to outshine her rivals. The Seymour family could not afford to commission elaborately jewelled and embroidered costumes. Instead, Jane's dresses expressed simplicity and modesty as their hallmarks. Queen Anne mocked her as a milkmaid come to court. But the king was impressed by Jane's maidenly virtue. Beside her the queen appeared showy and extravagant for every outfit she wore was more elaborate than the last. Queen Anne could not fathom why her elegance had lost its power to allure. But her daring French style was no longer a novelty at court. Her magnificence now appeared stately and overblown. Her detractors began to refer to her as "The Field of the Cloth of Gold."

The queen's mother, Lady Elizabeth, tried to counsel her. "The king has always taken mistresses. His first wife made little of the matter and in the end he lost interest. You are the queen. It is all that matters."

"It does matter, mother. It is a humiliation to me. His first wife's stubbornness delayed my marriage beyond all reason. And now the king's fickleness has ruined it. I wish that I had never married him."

"Hush, do not say so! Do not give in to provocation but always be calm and pleasant. Remember your queenly dignity!"

"What else do I have, mother, apart from my child?"

To console herself, Queen Anne designed splendid dresses for the two year old Princess Elizabeth who lived in her own establishment at Hatfield House. She ordered me to make a gown of orange velvet with a petticoat of russet velvet and a taffeta cap. She was determined to uphold her daughter's position and dressed her in the finest materials that could be obtained.

But not long afterwards there followed a most sombre day in the sewing room. Lady Lee berated us as a pack of gossips who cared nothing for the reputation of our betters. She announced that today we would work in silence while reflecting on the words of Ecclesiastes, "There is a time to be silent and a time to speak." Perhaps this would remind us to keep our wagging tongues still for once. I was mystified for this was most unlike the gracious Lady Lee. But I saw that some of the other seamstresses were not. Mary Dacre wore a knowing smirk and so at dinner I asked what had happened to provoke her. She was only too pleased to tell me the latest gossip.

"Haven't you heard? It's that Seymour creature. The king gave her a locket with his portrait as a token and she had the effrontery to open it in the presence of the queen. The queen was so provoked that she snatched it off her neck and broke the chain. She was left weeping and it has caused a great scandal in the court. The queen has demanded that the king send that Seymour woman from the court and he has refused. He told her that she must shut her eyes and endure as her betters have done before her. So Lady Lee is afraid that the queen is falling out of favour with the king and she doesn't want the servants talking about it. Soon we will be told to make an elaborate new dress for the queen to regain the king's attention. You see if I'm not right. But I'm glad that I don't serve in the queen's apartments for I'm told that she is quite beside herself and nothing can please her."

And Mary was entirely correct in her judgement, for the order for a new dress of white satin with a gold sash came the very next day. I was commissioned to cut out a pair of hanging sleeves of white satin and embroider them with purled gold acorns and honeysuckle flowers. In the language of courtly love the acorns represented King Henry and the honeysuckle flowers represented Queen Anne. The intricate design of the sleeves showed the intertwining of their mutual love. I expected that there would be a great occasion for the appearance of this special costume, either an anniversary or a court celebration at which a masque would be performed. But sad to say, this happy event was never to take place.

Queen Anne was distraught at the king's rejection for she was still a young and attractive woman and she retaliated by flirting with the gentlemen courtiers of her circle. Her eyes were her most attractive feature which she knew well now to use with effect. Sometimes leaving them at rest and at others sending a message to carry the secret witness of the heart. And such was their power that many surrendered to their fascination. In addition, she prided herself on her amusing and witty speech and took pleasure when they responded by vying with each other to pay her compliments. This recklessness eventually caused the downfall of all of them. Queen Anne did not realise that her games of courtly love created deadly danger for all those around her.

On one occasion, the queen had had reprimanded Sir Francis Weston for preferring her maid of honour Mistress Shelton to his wife, and he had answered that "he loved one in her house better than them both" When Anne asked who, he replied "It is yourself." Sir Francis then told her that Sir Henry Norris also came to her chamber more for her sake than for that of Madge Shelton. Intrigued, the queen asked Sir Henry why he was taking so long in courting her cousin Madge. When he replied that he "would tarry a time" she rebuked him, saying, "You look for dead men's shoes, for if aught came to the king but good, you would look to have me." His lordship was deeply shocked and replied that "If he should have any such thought he would his head were off." These careless remarks did not fail to come to the attention of the queen's adversaries.

But most disastrously, Mark Smeaton's success at the court had not failed to bring him enemies. There was much jealousy and many murmured about his wearing such fine dress when he was only a lowborn musician. The king and queen had both given him rich purses from time to time, and rather than saving it, he spent it on swords, horses and costumes so that he might look like a gentleman. A courtier named Thomas Percy sneered at him as an upstart who did not belong there. And the quarrel soon reached the ears of the queen who ordered him to be good friends with Mark and not to make trouble in court. He replied, "Madam, I have served you for many years and I will not be slighted by one who only came yesterday." This Thomas Percy was so provoked by the queen's great regard for Mark that he went to Master Cromwell and informed him that Mark was able to equip himself better than any other gentlemen of the court. Indeed, he had just bought three fine horses for the May Day jousts and everyone wondered where he had got the money. He said that on many occasions Mark had been to play in the queen's chamber and he recommended him to look to it. Master Cromwell told him to keep the matter a secret and to keep his eyes open to see who spoke to Mark.

And so the investigations soon began. It was alleged by one of Anne's ladies-in-waiting, Elizabeth Browne, that the queen *"admitted some of her court to come into her chamber at undue hours."* This was enough to cast suspicion upon all of her servants, especially those who had served in her private rooms. Mark became the main focus of the investigators. He was known to have sung and danced in the queen's own chambers and had drawn the interest of Master Cromwell's spies. One of them had reported a conversation between them in her room. She had asked why he looked so sad and he had replied that it was no matter. She had reminded him that he should not expect her to speak to him as she would to a nobleman, because he was an inferior. And Mark had replied, "No, no, Madam. A look suffieth." In his interrogation Mark was pressed to explain his meaning. And he admitted his feelings for the queen. This was enough to have him sent to the Tower of London and kept in irons on the charge of adultery. At this time, I was busy completing the queen's costumes for the tournament and the May Day festivities, so the spies did not identify me as one of Mark's associates.

When Master Cromwell's men, Thomas Wriothesley and Stephen Gardiner, came for me I made capital of my youth and ignorance. What could I know of the conversation of my betters? I was shut up in the sewing room all day long. Of course, I was not but Mistress Harvey confirmed it. She dared not appear to be lax in her duties. But many others were examined and condemned for what they knew. Some in their terror mouthed the very words that the examiners spoke to them. But I stubbornly persisted in my silence. Like most women of my class I could neither read nor write. Where would I have learned such things? Learning was a dangerous pastime at court. Better not to read books, nor write poems nor discuss matters of state and religion.

"Can you read and write?"

"No, my lord."

"Not even your own name?"

"No, my lord." In fact, Mark had taught me how to write my name. But I never paraded my knowledge. And so I could not be interrogated about anything I might have read.

"Are you a true Christian woman?"

"Yes, my lord."

"You know that it is a grave sin to lie."

"Yes, my lord. I know the Commandments."

"No more than that?"

"My father thought that was enough for a woman. "For Adam was created first, then Eve."" I had heard many disputes about what a Christian woman should know and they usually ended that way.

"Don't you wish to do your duty?"

"Yes, my lord. Lady Lee told me that I would be expected to sew a straight hem, fit sleeves and embroider shirts in black thread."

"Very commendable. And in the course of all this diligent sewing you heard no treasonable talk?"

"No, my lord. Mistress Harvey told us stories of the lives of the saints while we worked."

"And which saints might they be?"

"Saint George of England who slew a dragon."

"Leave her be. She's just a fool."

And so I escaped their malicious questions: "Who do you know? What did they say? Why did you not report this before?" For years I protected myself with the same story. Yes, I was at the court of King Henry, but as a mere servant I saw very little of the great events of the day. Believe me, the servants knew everything that went on at court. But fortunately, I was too insignificant to be worth a spy's attention.

Those days became a nightmare of terror. We maids were forbidden to speak to the queen and dared not speak to each other. Finally, the ever-resourceful Mary Dacre slid onto a bench beside me and broke the news to us in a whisper. "The queen's musician been taken to the Tower. There's no coming back from there. And he's a commoner. So he will be hung, drawn and quartered."

I couldn't bear the thought of it. "Don't say such things," I snapped and ran out of the room. I walked along the corridors pretending I was on an errand. A pall of gloom hung over everyone. There were no smiles, jokes or horseplay from the servers. Everyone walked around with their eyes on the ground. I went out into the palace grounds and looked up at Queen Anne's rooms. How was she feeling in the midst of this disaster? Mark was only the bait, but she was the prey.

During the May Day tournament at Greenwich Palace a message was delivered to the king and he immediately got up and left with his attendants. The letter was Master Cromwell's report of the confession of Mark Smeaton. On his way, the king called Sir Henry Norris over to him. He said he was suspected of having committed adultery with the queen and offered to pardon him if he confessed. Sir Henry protested that his relations with her had been perfectly innocent. Henry then rode away and Sir Henry was immediately arrested and kept a close prisoner. He was taken to the Tower by Sir William Fitzwilliam who tried hard to persuade him to confess that he was guilty. But Sir Henry declared that he *"would rather die a thousand deaths than accuse the queen of that which I believe her, in my conscience, innocent."* Afterwards, five other gentlemen of the court were arrested and questioned about their relationship with the queen. Sir Thomas Wyatt and Sir Richard Page were later released. But Sir Henry Norris, Sir Francis Weston, Sir William Brereton and George Boleyn were all charged with adultery and treason. The following morning while watching a tennis match Queen Anne was summoned to appear before several members of the Privy Council. She was accused of despising her marriage and entertaining malice against the king. And at the end of the interrogation she was also arrested and taken to the Tower.

CHAPTER 12:
THE LADY IN THE TOWER (1536)

After the arrest of the queen became known the atmosphere in the sewing room grew so tense that we jumped if anyone knocked on the door. Lady Lee set aside the making of costumes and set us to the plain sewing of linen. I asked permission to knit stockings as I found that it made my hands tremble less.

Suddenly there was a loud banging on the door. "Open for the king's guard and be quick about it!" We all froze in our places. Lady Lee courageously opened the door herself and was confronted by one of the guards from the Tower. He thrust a note at her saying, "You are ordered to send these clothes to the Lady in the Tower."

Lady Lee read the note and recovered some of her customary composure although she was deathly pale. "Certainly, Sir, I will attend to this matter myself. But I will have to enter the queen's chamber to obtain some of the items."

"Not you, my Lady," said the guard insolently. "Send one of these women here. Tell them what to fetch and then they can accompany me to the Tower."

We all stared down at the floor in horror at the idea. But I felt a sense of duty to the Boleyn family so I looked at Lady Lee and nodded. "I will go, Lady Lee."

She looked relieved. "Listen carefully, Margery. You are to go to the queen's chamber and bring two sets of undergarments, three pairs of woollen stockings and six frontlets for her hoods."

"Yes, Lady Lee. But they may not allow me to enter the queen's chamber."

The guard snatched the letter back and shoved it in my hand. "Show that to them!" he snapped. I hurried out of the room but surprisingly encountered no resistance to my request to fetch clothes for the queen. I wrapped it all inside a warm cloak and struggled back with the bundle to the sewing room.

Lady Lee insisted on checking the items despite the impatience of the guard. "I shall send some handkerchiefs as she is sure to need them." She wrapped up the bundle again and bade me take it carefully and send her best wishes to the queen.

The guard glowered at her. "Hurry girl or we shall miss the tide!"

And so I followed Queen Anne in her sorrowful journey by barge from Greenwich to the Tower. When we arrived at the iron gates my courage almost failed me, but I bit my lip and clutched my bundle close to me. The surly guard delivered me to the house of the Constable of the Tower, Sir William Kingston. "Come inside, girl," he said kindly. "You must be cold after your journey." And indeed, I was cold, but not from the river. "Lady Kingston will check the bundle and then we shall take it to your mistress." I sat on a stool by the fire and pretended to warm my hands, for my knees were trembling. Somewhere imprisoned in this great stone fortress were Queen Anne and poor Mark Smeaton. I shivered and Sir William gave me an encouraging look. "It is not far to go now and your mistress will be glad of the clothing. I have taken every care of her and she occupies the same rooms she did at her Coronation. I will escort you there myself." "Thank you, Sir William," I said gratefully and followed him along the corridors of the Tower. At every door we passed I wondered if Mark was kept within the cell. If only there was some way that I could let him know that I was here.

Finally, we arrived at a door with two guards who bowed respectfully to Sir William and opened the door. I was surprised to see such a fine apartment and so many attendant ladies. I recognised the queen's aunts, Lady Shelton and Lady Elizabeth Wood and her old nurse Mrs Mary Orchard who had lived with us at Hever.

"Kindly inform your mistress that her maid has brought her the clothing she requested, Mrs Stoner," said the Constable.

The reply soon came back, "The queen bids the maid bring her clothing to her chamber."

One of the ladies looked affronted. "I will check the bundle first, Sir William."

"There is no need, Mrs Coffin. Lady Kingston has already done so. You may take the bundle to your mistress and inform the guard when you are ready to leave. I bid you all good day, ladies."

And so it was that I was reunited with Queen Anne in her chamber in the Tower. She smiled ironically when she saw me. "So it is you that they sent, Margery." She looked around the room. "I entered here with more ceremony the last time I came."

"Yes, your Majesty," I replied as I placed the bundle onto the bed. I was surprised by how avidly the queen opened the bundle and sorted through the clothing.

"Did you bring any messages, Margery?" she whispered.

"No, your Majesty." I replied.

"What about paper and pen?"

"Just what was on the list, your Majesty."

She sighed. "Well it was worth a try. Do you have any news of my parents or the Princess Elizabeth."

"There has been no word, your Majesty."

Her eyes darkened with anger. "I have nothing with which to write and Sir William told me that if I had any message I could tell to him and he would send it on. So I dictated a letter to the king saying that if he has already determined of me, and that not only my death, but an infamous slander must bring him the enjoying of his desired happiness; then I desire of God, that he will not call him to a strict account for his unprincely and cruel usage of me. But I know not if he will have the courage to send it as he promised."

"I can take a message to Lady Lee, your Majesty," I assured her.

"You are a brave girl, Margery. There is one last service you can do for me. I am condemned although entirely innocent. It has all been done because the king has fallen in love with Jane Seymour and does not know how to get rid of me. But I do not care for all the harm they can do me now for they can never deny that I was a crowned queen. Tell Lady Lee to send you back with my robe of black damask, my cape of white ermine and my crimson petticoat for the day of my execution. They shall see me die as a queen and they will remember me."

"Yes, your Majesty. I will do it," I said.

She dropped her voice. "And there is one thing more. I would send a last message to my daughter Elizabeth. You must speak it only to my chaplain, Matthew Parker, and no other. You understand?"

"Yes, your Majesty."

"Tell her that as I sit here in the Tower all my thoughts are of her. And though I die condemned, yet I was a loyal and faithful wife to the king and his undoubted queen. And she is his true daughter and I commend her to show herself as his most affectionate and dutiful subject. And although the king will never acknowledge me, yet my friends who are known to Reverend Parker know the truth and will be mindful of her welfare and her spiritual care for my sake. And I am her most affectionate mother and she is constantly in my prayers."

I nodded but was too moved to speak. And at that moment one of the attendants came into the chamber. "Your pardon, my Lady, but the guards are waiting to escort the maid back to the palace. Why have you not put these clothes away, girl? What have you been doing all this time?" she demanded.

I had no idea what to say, but queen Anne remained as calm as a millpond. "I have instructed her what clothes she is to bring here for the day of my execution, Mrs Coffin. Do you remember, Margery?"

"Your black damask robe, your ermine cape and your crimson petticoat, your Majesty."

"That is well. You may go."

I curtsied and backed out of the chamber. As I passed by I saw Mrs Orchard and went to greet her.

"Be of good cheer, Mrs Orchard, so we might meet merrily again in Hever," I whispered in her ear.

"I am more like to meet again merrily in heaven, my dear girl. This tower is no place for old bones like mine."

"I will pray that we may all be reunited soon at our own castle, Mrs Orchard. So keep up your spirits."

Mrs Coffin interrupted us, her eyes narrow with suspicion. "Don't dawdle, girl. You are not here to gossip but only to follow orders. What else did the queen say to you in her bedroom?"

"That I am a brave girl, Mistress Coffin."

"And what else?"

"That I am to tell Lady Lee to send her black damask robe, ermine cape and crimson petticoat so that she may die as a queen."

Her face flushed red with anger. "We shall see what Sir William has to say about it," she snapped and banged on the door. "Open up," she shouted. "Take her back to the palace."

I stumbled out of the door and tried to keep up with the great strides of the guard. It occurred to me that I had missed my opportunity to speak about Mark to Sir William or the queen. Perhaps I could have sent him a message of good cheer. But now it was too late. I was brought to a boat tied up beside the gate and rowed back up the river to Greenwich. It was a cloudy day and I had no idea of the time. I wondered how I would manage to give the queen's message to her chaplain. The palace was full of spies and I might be questioned again about my visit to the Tower. Finally, I arrived back at the Palace of Greenwich in a most gloomy mood. I made my way to the sewing room and to my surprise found only Lady Lee waiting there in a state of great anxiety. "What a time you have been, Margery! Was it very terrible?"

"Yes, Lady Lee. It is a dreadful place."

"I have sent the others away. Did you complete your errand? And did you see the queen?"

"Yes, Lady Lee. She was glad of the clothes. And she wishes you to send me back with her black damask robe, ermine cape and crimson petticoat."

"Did she say why?"

"She intends to wear them on the day of her execution so that she may die in the estate of a queen."

At these words, Lady Lee lost her composure and began to weep. "My poor lady, my dear friend. Then there is no hope left for you."

I sat on the bench and laid my head on the table for I was exhausted by the day's events. Silent tears streamed down my face. Lady Lee at once composed herself and began fussing over me. "My poor girl, what a terrible ordeal for you. I shall get you some soup and hot wine for indeed you must be chilled. We must not despair, even now. And we shall fulfill her last request. I will prepare her clothes myself so that she may take comfort in her royal rank on her last day. I will find a trusted page to bear them in a chest but you shall take her shoes and perhaps you may have the chance to speak with her again. You will eat and rest now and leave all the arrangements to me."

"Yes, Lady Lee," I said gratefully. But when I had eaten, I made my way to the chapel. I knew I could not rest until I had completed my errand. After all, I could still be arrested and questioned at any time. I arrived in time for Vespers and reminded myself that it was entirely fitting for me to attend the daily offices of the church. During the service I prayed sincerely for Mark, for Queen Anne and for the Princess Elizabeth to be delivered from their peril. And afterwards, I asked one of the ushers if I could speak to his Reverence, Father Parker. "What do you wish to speak about, Mistress?" he enquired. "I wish to ask for his spiritual advice, Sir," I replied. I knew he was not supposed to refuse me, but these were strange times. I waited a considerable time and finally he came to see me. Fortunately, he recognised me as one of the servants from Hever, but he still looked doubtful. I could not blame him for even the most trusted friends had broken faith and the interrogations were continuing. I gathered my courage. "Please hear my confession, Father Parker."

"Come with me, Mistress Hallows," he replied. I followed him to the confessional.

"Bless me, Father, for I have sinned. It has been a month since my last confession."

"What sins have you committed since then?"

"I have despaired of the goodness of God, Father Parker."

He sighed. "These are trying times. But we must never lose sight of the goodness of God or relinquish the comfort of prayer. Our Lord stands ready to assist us with his grace at all times."

"Yes, Father Parker. And there is a lady known to us both who much desires your care for her daughter. I saw her today when I took her some clothes. She said that I am to speak these words only to you."

"Speak on, my daughter."

"The lady says that as she waits all her thoughts are of her daughter. And though she be condemned yet she was a loyal and faithful wife to the king. And his undoubted queen. And she is his true daughter and she does commend her to show herself as his most affectionate and dutiful subject. And although the king will never acknowledge her, yet my friends who are known to you know the truth and they will be mindful of her welfare and her spiritual care for her sake. And she is her most affectionate mother and keeps her constantly in her prayers."

"Is there anything more, my daughter?"

"That is all, Father Parker."

"I believe you, Mistress Hallows, for the lady spoke to me in a similar vein just six days prior to her arrest. I will assuredly stand a friend to her daughter and give her this message when she reaches the age of understanding. In the meantime, I absolve you of your sins and bid you go in peace. And I shall pray for them."

"Bless you, Father Parker. And please pray for my friend Mark for I am most fearful for him."

He frowned. "Do not speak of him again, Mistress Hallows. It is not safe. And when you can leave here you should make your way back to Hever for it will be the only sanctuary open to you."

"Thank you for your goodness to my lady, Father Parker. I shall trouble you no more and I bid you goodnight."

"Farewell, daughter, and take care how you speak. These are dangerous times."

I curtseyed and walked as quickly as I dared to my dormitory. Fortunately, the other maids had not yet retired and so I was spared their questions.

The following afternoon, Lady Lee sent for me to come to her room. "It is all arranged," she said quietly. "You will be permitted to take some more clothes to Queen Anne and a page will accompany you there. If you are able to see the queen, then tell her that her friends are all hoping for a happy resolution and her speedy return to us."

"Yes, Lady Lee. I will tell her if I see her."

But on this occasion, I was not permitted to see Queen Anne nor did I meet Sir William Kingston again. One of the guards took us directly to the queen's apartment and the hateful Mrs Coffin opened the door. "So, the little chatterbox is back here already? There is no need for you to enter this time. Boy, bring in that chest and open it so that I may check the contents."

I tried to protest. "Lady Lee desires the queen to satisfy herself that everything is according to her wishes. These are her personal royal clothes and they are most valuable."

She ignored me and tried to shut the door in my face. I quickly thrust my arm clutching a leather bag through the gap. "These are the queen's shoes," I cried out. She seized them and then abruptly closed the door. Shortly afterwards, the page was ushered outside and we were left without a word of thanks. I could see from his black looks that the page resented this discourteous treatment and I pinched his arm. "Please take us back to the palace so that we may report to Lady Lee that we have fulfilled our orders," I asked the guard. We both seethed in silence all the way back upriver. As soon as we landed and the boatmen were out of earshot the page let loose his pent up fury. "That dreadful woman tumbled the queen's clothes onto the floor. Then she said that they would fetch a pretty price for Sir William and they were his perquisite as the Constable of the Tower."

"We have done our duty the best that we could. And the queen has got her clothes now. Lady Lee will be relieved to hear it."

We related our sorry tale to Lady Lee who looked most grieved. "I had hoped that you would be able to see her one last time and give her a message of good cheer. Tell no-one else of your errand lest you be reported as friends of the queen. If anyone should ask, then you simply did your duty as good servants."

There were no more visits to the Tower. On 15th May Queen Anne was brought to trial in the King's Hall in the Tower. She admitted giving presents to Sir Francis Weston but denied the accusation of treason. Her own uncle, the Duke of Norfolk, pronounced her guilty of all charges and sentenced her to death. Queen Anne then declared, "I do not say that I have always borne towards the king the humility which I owed him. I admit too, that I have often taken it into my head to be jealous of him. But may God be my witness if I have done him any other wrong. As for my brother and the other gentlemen who are unjustly condemned, I would willingly die to save them; but as that is not the king's pleasure, I shall accompany them in death. And then afterwards, I shall live in eternal peace and joy without end, where I shall pray to God for the king and for you, my lords."

On May 17th the news came that Sir George Boleyn, Sir Henry Norris, Sir Francis Weston, Sir William Brereton and Mark Smeaton had all been beheaded on a scaffold on Tower Hill. We knew it would not been long now until the queen herself would die. Rumour said that her execution had been delayed because the king had sent for an expert swordsman to come all the way from St Omer in France. Then Lady Lee received a message to attend Queen Anne as her Mistress of the Robes. I was glad for now I knew that she would have a friend beside her and would be attired in the proper manner. On 19th May the rumour spread through the court that the cannons along Tower Wharf had been fired as a signal that Queen Anne had been executed that morning.

The following day Lady Lee returned to the Palace of Greenwich and she sent for me. I was shocked by her appearance for she looked as wasted as if she had suffered a long illness. She was holding a beautiful Book of Hours in her hands. "Come and see this Margery," she said. "It is her last message to us."

"I cannot read, Lady Lee."

"Then I will read it to you, Margery. "Remember me when you do pray, that hope doth lead from day to day." She gave it to me on the scaffold. And she wore the royal dress that she had chosen. I put it on her myself. She never looked more beautiful nor more queenly. And she died without pain. The executioner was very quick. However, no one had thought to provide a coffin so her body was left to lie upon the scaffold. It was left to us poor ladies to clean her body, wrap it in a white cloth and place it into an arrow chest for we did not want her to be handled by men in an unworthy way. Then she was buried in an unmarked grave in the Chapel Royal of St Peter ad Vincula in the Tower. And may she rest there in peace and rise in glory."

"Amen. I am glad that you were with her at the last, Lady Lee."

"So am I for now I am her witness that she spoke well and died most bravely. To the ladies who accompanied her she said, "As I cannot reward you for your true service to me, I pray you take comfort for my loss. Esteem your honour far above your life, and in prayers forget not to pray for my soul." But to me she confided "Do not think that I am sorry to die, or that I have done anything to deserve this death. I say to you all that everything they have accused me of is false, and the principal reason I am to die is Jane Seymour."

"I know well that she was innocent, Lady Lee. And I also know that on the day of her execution the king rode out to meet Jane Seymour. May God forgive them both."

"To the crowd she spoke her last words, "Good Christian people, I am come hither to die, for according to the law, and by the law I am judged to die, and therefore I will speak nothing against it. I am come hither to accuse no man, or to speak anything of that whereof I am accused and condemned to die, but I pray God save the king and send him long to reign over you, for a gentler, nor a more merciful prince was there never, and to me he was ever a good, a gentle, and a sovereign Lord. And if any person will meddle of my cause, I require them to judge the best. And thus I take my leave of the world, and of you all, and I heartily desire you all to pray for me." Then she took off her mantle and her hood and tucked her hair under a linen cap. And as she knelt and prayed the whole crowd knelt and prayed with her and so she met a most Christian end. I wanted you to know of her final moments for now her household will be broken up and we may not meet again. I intend to retire from the court for Queen Anne was like a sister to me and I do not wish to serve as Mistress of the Robes to another in her place. I wish that I could take you with me, Margery. But I will lose my salary from the court and it will make a significant difference to my family. I hope that you will find a good place for you were a faithful servant of the queen. But that will not help you now."

"I am grateful for all your kindness to me, Lady Lee. And I will not be sorry to leave the court." I spoke truly for the loss of poor Mark and my unfortunate mistress had left me with no more desire to stay. I now understood the meaning of the ominous words *"circa Regna tonat"* (thunder rolls around the throne). And yet my mind still turns back to the memory of a long-ago spring day when King Henry rode out in joy beside his true love to dedicate his latest ship, the Anne Gallant. In those days he considered her a gallant lady and wanted to whole world to know it too. Her smile was all the reward he needed. He gave her all the gifts that a devoted king could give his lady, including raising her up to be his queen. And on the day of her coronation she took as her motto; "La Plus Heureuse." But these happy memories were outweighed by the darker ones – her miscarriages, her ambitions and her jealous rages. He raised her up and then he cast her down. And afterwards he ordered all her portraits destroyed, her emblems re-carved, her very memory obliterated. So all that now remains is her ship, the Anne Gallant.

CHAPTER 13:
Aftermath (1537-1539)

Lady Lee was not mistaken in her predictions. Only eleven days after the death of Queen Anne, King Henry VIII married the lady Jane Seymour. The court seamstresses were ordered to create a royal wardrobe for the new queen. But that did not include me for Queen Jane preferred the English fashions to the French style favoured by Queen Anne. The late queen's servants were commanded to pack up their chests and depart from the court, for the king no longer required their service. When I collected my box from the sewing room I saw pity in the eyes of the others. But Mary Dacres' eyes gleamed with spite. "Such a shame that French fashions are no longer popular here. Will you go to serve at the French court, Margery?" I didn't bother to answer her. My own loss seemed little enough compared to the six victims who had suffered execution at the hands of a vengeful king.

I had heard that the property of traitors was confiscated by the Crown. So I made up my mind to fetch Mark's lute from the music room. It was his own property from Flanders and I was his only remaining friend. My heart was hammering as I made my way along the corridors to the music room. It was a place used only by the court musicians and I had no plausible reason for entering. But I was in luck and the music room was deserted. I soon spotted the lute hanging from a wooden peg and concealed it under my cloak. Back in the dormitory I tied it up carefully in a length of green silk and hid it at the bottom of my chest. However, the goods of all departing courtiers and servants were being carefully searched by the Sergeant at Arms and his men. I decided that I would have to take a risk. When it was my turn, I surreptitiously offered the king's gift to the soldier on duty. "It's real silver," I said. "And there is nothing of interest in my chest." It quickly disappeared into his sleeve and he pasted the seal of red wax across the lid.

Apart from securing Mark's lute, I hardly cared what happened to me. By this time all my brothers and sisters had married. My father had died and my oldest brother had inherited the farm. He had a family of three children and was not likely to welcome a disgraced sister whom he had not seen for the past fourteen years. I decided to return to service with the Boleyn family at Hever Castle. Queen Anne's parents, Sir Thomas and Lady Elizabeth, were exiles from the court just like me. So I joined their retinue for the sad journey back to Kent. It pleased me to see Mrs Orchard among the company. I took up the post of housekeeper, as dear Mistress Carew was now too feeble for such an energetic role. I organised the household linen and took over the management of simples and preserves in the stillroom. There was no need for the making of fine court dresses in their household. But the life had gone out of the house for none of their children or grandchildren lived with them. First Lady Elizabeth died and then Sir Thomas. Their surviving daughter Mary inherited their estate at Rochford. Only Anne's elderly grandmother Lady Margaret Boleyn remained at the castle. When she died, the estate reverted to the Crown and I wondered whom I would serve now?

CHAPTER 14:

Service to Lady Anne of Cleves (1540-1557)

By an extraordinary turn of fortune Hever was given to the Lady Anne of Cleves, the divorced fourth wife of King Henry. Their separation was amicable for she agreed to live as the king's good sister and he rewarded her with houses and rents so that she might live as befitted a former queen. The steward of Hever stood my friend and recommended me to the Lady Anne of Cleves as a famous dressmaker at the royal court. In her household I was reminded of my youth in the service of the Boleyn family before they had taken their children to court and vied for the favour of the king. We all admired the wisdom of the Lady Anne who spoke no words in his dispraise, but kept her own counsel. She was a good mistress who kept a well-ordered house and treated her servants considerately. In her homeland the virtuous ladies of Cleves were instructed in the domestic arts rather than accomplishments, but she took delight not only in entertaining visitors but in enjoying the forbidden pleasures of playing games of cards and dancing. Everyone esteemed her as an amiable lady who loved all the English fashions and lived a merry life. She enjoyed the freedom of an English noblewoman and journeyed between her properties at Richmond Palace, Bletchingley Manor and Hever Castle like a great aristocrat. Several times the king came to dine with her as a sign of his regard. However, I never laid eyes on him again for I blamed him for the deaths of young Mark and the destruction of the Boleyn family which had pulled my life down with them.

The Lady Anne of Cleves made occasional visits to court to meet ambassadors or exchange New Year gifts but was content to live a quiet and dignified life far away from the intrigues of the rival noble houses. We were all shocked to hear the news in February 1542 that the king's fifth wife Catherine Howard had been taken to the Tower and executed on the charge of adultery. It reminded me of the horrors I had experienced at the royal court as the servant of the accused Queen Anne. The servants of the household muttered together that it was a judgement upon the king for setting aside the Lady Anne of Cleves for so little cause. There was talk that now he might come to a better appreciation of her qualities and take her back as his wife. However, nothing came of this suggestion and in July 1543 the king married the widowed Catherine Parr as his sixth wife. King Henry VIII died in January 1547 and was succeeded by his nine year old son Edward VI. The Lady Anne of Cleves and her household wore mourning out of respect, but I suspected that they were as relieved as I was by his passing. Now that he had gone from our lives we could spend our time in peace and safety. The Lady Anne had an abiding love of new dresses and being an accomplished needlewoman she liked nothing better than to sit and discuss them with me. One day as I was sewing in her rooms she asked me an unexpected question. "Mistress Hallows, do you not intend to marry?"

I was taken aback. "It is kind of you to think of me, Lady Anne. But I am thirty-seven and long past the age of marrying."

"Older than I, but not too old for marriage. I cannot remarry, of course. It would not look well and besides I have everything I need."

"It is the same with me, Lady Anne. What more do I need?"

"More than just a life of faithful service, I think. We both left our youth behind us at the Tudor court, but many royal servants have married and prospered. If there was a man of my household who found favour with you, then I would give you a dowry."

The foolish tears welled up in my eyes. I could not help it. If only Queen Anne had said those words to me then I might have been happy and safe together with Mark.

"I did not mean to grieve you, my dear," said Lady Anne. "You will think on what I said?"

"Yes, my Lady. I am most grateful." But I knew that I would never marry now. I had met no one who could compare with the memory of Mark. In these great households there were men who were prudent, capable and practical, men of whom my father would have approved, and who were more suited to my own personality. I could clearly see Mark's faults in retrospect for he was rash, vain and extravagant. And yet no one else's voice enchanted me like his and no one else's eyes conveyed such passion for life. Perhaps it was foolish of me, but I liked to think that in time he would have realised the folly of his passion for Queen Anne and married within his own degree.

What caused the downfall of Anne and Mark, I wondered? The jealousies of the Tudor court? The ruthless determination of Henry to have a son at any cost? Or their own foolish ambitions which led them into danger? The Lady Anne of Cleves was wiser for she understood how to bend with the wind, to outlast the storm and to find lasting happiness. If I had never gone to court I would have escaped the greatest joy and disaster of my life. I would have lived a peaceful and useful life at Hever. But somehow I missed my chance at happiness, for I was marked forever by the romantic dreams of Anne and Mark and their terrible consequences. It made me mistrust the glittering pathways of ambition and love. Perhaps I simply lacked the courage to pursue my dreams as they did.

CHAPTER 15:
The Virgin Queen (1558) (1558-1603)

My good mistress Lady Anne of Cleves died in July 1557 and was given a royal funeral at Westminster Abbey. She bequeathed each of her servants a year's wages and black cloth for their mourning clothes and her household was dispersed. Hever Castle reverted back to the Crown and became the property of Sir Edward Waldegrave. Again, I wondered whom I would serve? And yet again, good fortune stepped in. The following year the childless Queen Mary Tudor died and her half-sister Elizabeth Tudor came to the throne. Her treasurer, Sir Thomas Parry, was appointed as controller of her household and sought out her mother's family and friends for preferment. Some of them, including her aunt Mary Stafford and Lady Margaret Lee, had already died. But others, such as her Boleyn cousins Henry and Catherine Carey, were invited to court to attend the coronation of the new queen. There were few former servants of the Boleyn family left at Hever. However, Sir Thomas Parry dispatched his servant John Tamworth to Hever to advise on how best to dispose of us. Most were pensioned off as being too old for future service. But when he questioned me, I sensed his interest.

"You say you were the dressmaker to both Queen Anne and then the Lady Anne of Cleves?" he asked imperturbably.

"Yes indeed, Sir."

"Can anyone vouch for you?"

"I do not know anyone at the court now, Sir."

"I see," he said, raising an eyebrow. I could tell that he thought that I was exaggerating my importance. But when the time came for him to leave I was invited to accompany him and present myself to Sir Thomas Parry. The household of the new queen was gathering at the Palace of Westminster for the Christmas court. We arrived in London the day after the funeral of Queen Mary at Westminster Abbey, and I was told to find a place in the women's dormitory and await my summons from him. After two days, a page came in search of me and brought me to his apartment. Sir Thomas was a large set man with shrewd grey eyes. "So, you are Mistress Hallows. I hear that you claim to be a former servant of the Boleyn family."

"Yes, Sir Thomas. I was born on the estate of Hever and I came to serve in the household of Sir Thomas Boleyn and Lady Elizabeth at the age of ten."

He looked me over carefully. "That is likely, that is likely," he muttered. "In what capacity did you serve, Mistress Hallows."

"As an assistant housekeeper and then as dressmaker to their daughter, Queen Anne."

"And in what year did you come to court, Mistress Hallows?"

"In the year 1523, Sir Thomas."

"I see. After a space of thirty-five years I am not likely to find any who would remember your service, Mistress Hallows."

"No, Sir Thomas. It is so long since I was last at court that I can recognise no-one. Indeed, I never thought to see the court again."

"Well, you have the true accent of Kent, Mistress Hallows. It would be a pity to bring you so far and not test your skill. So I shall send you to see Mistress Catherine Ashley, the Mistress of the Queen's Wardrobe. She is the best person to determine your abilities."

"Thank you for your interest, Sir Thomas," I say as I make my curtsey. "I will do my best not to disappoint Mistress Ashley."

“The queen is loyal to her faithful servants, Mistress Hallows. I have appointed thirty-eight new members of the queen’s household already. So, one more will not go amiss.” He waved his hand and I backed out of the door to the waiting pageboy. He looked at me quizzically.

“You are to escort me to Mistress Ashley,” I informed him.

“She is in the queen’s Privy Chamber, Mistress,” he said apologetically. “The Yeomen of the Guard will not let you enter there.”

“But they will let you enter, won’t they?” I counter. “It is the order of Sir Thomas Parry.”

He flinched and complied. “Come with me, Mistress.” I followed him through a series of splendid apartments to a door which was attended by a tall guard in red livery. As the page had predicted, he refused to allow me to pass through the door. But he did permit the page to take a message to Mistress Ashley. I stood and waited patiently with a crowd of other petitioners until a woman appeared at the door and spoke to the guard. The page stepped out and whispered to me that I was now permitted to enter. I followed her into the Privy Chamber where I saw a number of ladies in waiting. I wondered if I was going to have an audience with the queen. But she led me into a side room where I saw the familiar sight of a sewing table. It was set out with embroidery frames, a pair of shears, pins, needles and silk threads supplied by the silk woman. Mistress Ashley was a woman of mature age with large dark eyes. She sat on the opposite side of the table and looked at me keenly. “I understand that you claim to have served as the court dressmaker to Queen Anne, Mistress Hallows?”

“Yes, Mistress Ashley,” I murmured. “And then I was in service to the Lady Anne of Cleves.”

“That may be, Mistress Hallows,” she retorted. “I was a friend to Queen Anne and she entrusted me with the care of her daughter Queen Elizabeth. Who can verify your claim to be a loyal servant of the Boleyn’s?”

An old memory stirred in my mind. “There might be one person, Mistress

Ashley. Father Matthew Parker was one of Queen Anne's chaplains. I think he would remember me if he is still here at court."

Mistress Ashley gazed at me wide-eyed. "Father Parker is well known to us. And Queen Elizabeth intends to reward him for his good service by appointing him as her Archbishop of Canterbury. What else can you tell me. Did you ever meet any members of Princess Elizabeth's household?"

I shook my head. "I never visited Hatfield House, Mistress Ashley. But I did make dresses for the little princess. Queen Anne commissioned a gown of orange velvet with a petticoat of russet velvet when she was two years of age."

"Two years," mused Mistress Ashley. "Princess Elizabeth was then in the care of Lady Margaret Bryan, the governess before me. But Lady Bryan is long gone and I doubt that anyone else would remember it now. However, I will take your tale to the queen." She rose and went out in search of her mistress. When she returned again she looked at me with approval. "The queen says she remembers her mother's gift, Mistress Hallows."

"She can't possibly remember it, Mistress Ashley," I blurted out without thinking. "She was much too young at the time."

"It would surprise you what the queen can remember, Mistress Hallows," said Mistress Ashley with pride. "She would like to see you, so come with me."

I followed Mistress Ashley into the queen's bedchamber which was dominated by a regal bed with a crimson satin headboard and luxurious quilts of silk and velvet under a red canopy of state. And there I saw Queen Elizabeth, the last of the Boleyn's – and the last of the Tudors. She was a slight young woman with her father's striking red hair, but the dark eyes and oval face of her mother. She wore a dress of black velvet bordered with pearls and a black mantle as a sign of respect for her sister, the late Queen Mary. We both made deep curtsies before her.

"Your Majesty, this is Mistress Hallows who was the dressmaker to your mother, Queen Anne."

"Mistress Hallows, you have been recommended to us as a faithful servant of the Boleyn family."

"I served them for nineteen years, your Majesty."

"And afterwards you were the dressmaker to the Lady Anne of Cleves?"

"Yes, your Majesty. I served her for seventeen years."

"It is said that you have a remarkable talent for making royal costumes."

"I have made a great many over the years, your Majesty. I made the dress for the coronation of Queen Anne."

"Do you design as well as sew, Mistress Hallows?"

"I follow the instructions of my mistresses, your Majesty. They have a vision for a dress and I make it for them."

She gave me an appraising look. I saw that she liked the idea. The Tudors value talent in a servant, but too much initiative is seen as presumptuous. "Can you write, Mistress Hallows."

"No, your Majesty. I was trained in the art of sewing from childhood."

She smiled slightly. For some reason, literacy in a servant is not considered desirable. "Are you married, Mistress Hallows?"

"No, your Majesty. I had not the inclination. I have devoted my life to the service of both my mistresses."

She smiled warmly. Queen Elizabeth was known as "The Virgin Queen." And she had a strong conviction that royal service was a higher calling than marriage. "You shall stay with us for a time, Mistress Hallows. Perhaps we shall find a use for your talents."

"Thank you, your Majesty," I said as I curtsey and walk backwards out of the room. I presumed she meant to make a trial of my aptitude. Mistress Ashley followed me out and led me back to the door of the Privy Chamber.

"Who told you to say that?" she asked me.

"What do you mean, Mistress Ashley?" I replied.

"Never mind. You may return to your dormitory now, Mistress Hallows. You will be summoned if you are needed." She turned and walked away. The door closed behind her and the guard fixed me with a hard stare. I stepped away and made my way back to the dormitory. My head was in a whirl and my hands were trembling. I was much older than when I first came to court, but it was just as overwhelming. I had no appetite. I sat on my bed and tried to block out the insistent memories of the past. I hardly slept at all that night.

The next morning, the page brought a summons to the sewing room and this time the guard allowed me to pass through the door. Mistress Ashley introduced me to the four court seamstresses. They were all young women and none of them were familiar to me. I wondered what happened to the ones I knew, but most likely they married and retired from court long ago. To my surprise, there were also two men whom Mistress Ashley introduced as the Queen's Embroiderer, David Smyth, and his assistant, William Middleton. "Master Smyth and Master Middleton are both members of the Guild of Broderers, Mistress Hallows." Her maid placed a basket on the table which contained a collection of fine kid gloves. "The queen wishes to give these gloves as New Year's gifts to her ladies in waiting," said Mistress Ashley to us. "You are to embroider them with suitable designs. There are skeins of silk of all colours and gold and silver thread."

It is a task that I had done many times. I reflected upon the devices of different ladies of the court. The pomegranate of Queen Catherine of Aragon. The white falcon of Queen Anne. And the phoenix of Queen Jane. I wondered what emblem would best please Queen Elizabeth? I had not yet had time to study her tastes. I decided that a classic Tudor rose of red upon white on a background of shaded green leaves could not fail to impress. The next day I was asked to embroider the same rose design on a pair of black velvet slippers. The same request followed for a frontlet for a white hood and then a pair of white sleeves. I know who is commissioning these items. Evidently my selection of a Tudor rose design was a happy choice.

Mistress Ashley took me aside for a private word. She looked impressed and I guessed that my trial was complete. "The queen wishes to speak to you," she informed me. Queen Elizabeth liked to spend her mornings in the Privy Chamber where she would deal with her correspondence, take her meals and receive foreign visitors. The walls were hung with fine tapestries and the floor was spread with carpets worked in Turkish knots. The queen was sitting on a chair covered with red damask and cushions embroidered with gold thread below a canopy of state. She nodded graciously as I approached and made my curtsey. "Mistress Hallows, we hope that you are comfortable here at the court. I have a vision for a new dress which I would like you to make in time for the Christmas court. It shall be a robe made from black velvet set with roses of gold and rows of pearls. The other seamstresses will assist you in this task."

"It would be a great honour, your Majesty." I curtsied and returned to the sewing room where I explained the queen's commission to Mistress Ashley.

"Yes indeed, Mistress Hallows," she remarked. "The queen prefers to dress in black and white colours to represent virginity and purity."

"I shall be ready to make whatever costumes please her Majesty," I replied.

"It will be good to have another mature woman in service here, Mistress Hallows," said Mistress Ashley approvingly. "The queen has a strong preference for appointing candidates who are young and beautiful at court. You know, she refused to give a place to a man just because he was missing a tooth. But the queen was most pleased with your embroidery. You are to receive a salary of twenty five pounds a year as a court seamstress together with your livery and bouge of court."

I expressed my thanks to Mistress Ashley for my appointment. But my wage was not much more than I received in the time of Queen Anne over twenty years ago. I realised that Queen Elizabeth is no more munificent than her mother, although she is equally concerned about her dress and her image. I wondered in what other ways she will show herself to be her daughter? Over the next days and weeks I was busy preparing the queen's Christmas dress. Mistress Ashley was equally preoccupied in supervising the ladies in waiting to make a catalogue of the crown jewels on behalf of the queen. I found that the other young seamstresses were pleasant girls. It was a better role than being one of the queen's chamberers whose duties are to clean and launder. The queen's embroiderers were dignified men who are most serious about their craft.

One day Master Smyth condescended to explain his views to me. "We have established a guild of broderers, Mistress Hallows, so that our skills may be taught to apprentices and preserved. In this way, the standards of our craft may be maintained and upheld. And of course, the standards of the royal court are far superior to any other household in the land. There is no place for amateurs in our ranks, no matter how gifted. Only the masters know all the secrets of the craft. It has taken many years for me to gain my standing in the guild."

I glanced over at his hands. He had the large, strong fingers of a man which cannot possibly compare with the small fingers of a woman. I began to learn to sew at the age of four because everyone knows that the best embroiderers are children. They had the sharpest eyesight and the nimblest fingers for delicate stitching. However, they lack the skills and stamina to master the complicated art of dressmaking. I realised that Master Smyth regarded me as a rival to his own position when I overheard him commenting to Mistress Ashley that my designs are old-fashioned and provincial as a result of my being so long absent from the royal court. He offered to supervise me in the correct mode of patterns and suitable decorative art. However, Mistress Ashley informed Master Smyth that the queen made her own decisions about her wardrobe. It was for her to decide what she will wear and who will make it. Afterwards, Mistress Ashley showed considerable diplomacy in assigning separate projects to Master Smyth which included the queen's bedspreads, bed curtains and wall hangings. And I admit that they did look splendid when they were completed.

Fortunately, his assistant Master Middleton was more approachable. He is a younger man with dark blonde hair and blue eyes. One day he asked me a question. "Where did you learn your craft, Mistress Hallows?"

"I learned my skills from my grandmother, Master Middleton. There is a long tradition of sewing and knitting in our part of Kent."

"Your embroidery is a marvel of skill, Mistress Hallows. If you were a man then you would be one of the leading lights of our guild."

"It has taken me a lifetime to master the art of royal dressmaking, Master Middleton. A guild is a good idea for training new apprentices. But I would hope that those who are unconnected to the guildsmen would also have the opportunity to become members if they have the talent."

He shook his head. "In practice, Mistress Hallows, the skills of the guildsmen are passed on from father to son. It is a protection for craftsmen so that their services may be properly valued and rewarded. It takes much sacrifice and dedication to reach the standing of a master."

"Are you a master broderer like Master Smyth?" I asked.

"At present I am a freeman of the guild and I work as an assistant to Master Smyth. We are both expert in the art of gold and silver threadwork and blackwork embroidery. But I hope that I shall succeed in being named a liveryman by the other members of the guild. Service at the royal court is a great opportunity for any guildsman to make their name and fortune."

His words reminded me of poor Mark Smeaton who once hoped that his talents would make his fortune at court. "Talent is only enough to gain the notice of a patron, Master Middleton. The best servants learn the art of pleasing their masters so well that they keep them in their service for a lifetime."

"And how have you learned to please in the course of your service, Mistress Hallows?"

"It is about making a study of their tastes. My first mistress, Queen Anne, introduced the French style to the royal court and aspired to be the leader of fashion. And my second mistress, the Lady Anne of Cleves, adopted the English style in preference to that of her homeland but was most particular that her dress always conveyed her status as the king's sister. As royal dressmakers we are the caretakers of their prestige and image. It is a heavy responsibility, Master Middleton."

"And what of our current mistress, Queen Elizabeth?"

"She desires that her dress should be sufficiently splendid to demonstrate her position as a ruling monarch. And that it expresses her feminine attractions at the centre of a court which is notable for its handsome young men and women. I believe that she will soon be setting the fashion for all others to follow."

The celebrations for the Christmas court took place at the Palace of Whitehall which had once been known as York Place. It was the largest palace in Europe with over fifteen hundred rooms and the main residence of the queen. Its walls and galleries were lined with magnificent paintings, tapestries and statues from all around the world. The queen's choristers assembled in the Great Hall and opened the festivities by singing before the court:

"So now is come our joyful'st feast,
Let every man be jolly.
Each room with ivy leaves is drest,
And every post with holly.
Though some churls at our mirth repine,
Round your foreheads garlands twine,
Drown sorrow in a cup of wine,
And let us all be merry."

Queen Elizabeth was presented with her first pair of knitted silk stockings from Italy by her silk woman Alice Montague. They pleased her so much that she declared that they were pleasant, fine and delicate and henceforth she would wear no other kind. Mistress Ashley took care that the queen's servants should enjoy their own revelry by providing a festive bowl of spiced ale with roasted apples, a plate of marchpane and a fine Christmas cake containing a hidden bean and pea. Much to our delight Master Middleton was chosen as the King of the Bean and young Abigail Heveningham as his Queen of the Pea. They led us in singing, dancing, jesting and paying forfeits. When it was my turn Master Middleton approached me and requested that I danced with him. It had been many long years since I had last danced with Mark. But I found that I had not forgotten the way of it. "Mistress Hallows," whispered Master Middleton. "I would that you had been chosen as the queen!" It was the merriest Christmas that I could remember at court.

CHAPTER 16:

GLORIANA (1559)

The first great occasion of the queen's reign was her coronation in January 1559. The coronation robe of the late Queen Mary was adjusted to fit Queen Elizabeth who was taller and more slender. It was a robe made from cloth of gold and silver, overlaid with gold lace and trimmed with ermine. I was also commissioned to make a mantel of embroidered silk lined with ermine due to the inclement weather. The queen's faithful servants Mistress Ashley and Blanche Parry took places of honour in the coronation procession. It was a magnificent spectacle intended to impress the people with the renown of their new sovereign. As they processed through the streets of London she stopped to accept bouquets of flowers, purses of coins and even a humble sprig of rosemary from her well-wishers. And she told the crowds, "Be assured that I will be as good unto you as ever a queen was to her people."

Following the coronation ceremony, many further commissions for dresses followed. The queen cultivated a glittering court which required a variety of gowns for her official receptions with ambassadors and foreign visitors. At the end of January the queen made a ceremonial procession from the palace of Whitehall to Westminster Abbey for the opening of Parliament. She wore a majestic crimson robe, a round cape of ermine and a golden cap. In May the queen received an embassy from France bringing a peace treaty between the two nations. She invited them for supper at the palace of Whitehall where the Master of the Revels had erected a banqueting house in the garden hung with gold and silver brocade. She wore a dress of purple velvet adorned with gold, pearls and jewels to emphasise her royal status. During the banquet the company were entertained with music and afterwards they danced until late into the night. It reminded me of the long-ago nights of revelry that I had known in the court of the queen's parents. In June the queen commissioned a portrait of herself to send as a gift to King Henri II of France. It showed her wearing a red satin gown interwoven with gold thread and studded with diamonds.

In addition, the queen required costumes for the court masques for her wardrobe. The themes of the masques were often tales of gods and goddesses from mythology. At Shrovetide Queen Elizabeth wore a white silk gown decorated with pearls and bordered with silver lace and a mantle of black silk shot through with silver threads. She was entertained at Whitehall Palace by a masque of "Diana and her Nymphs" performed by six nymphs dressed in cloth of silver and eight maidens in purple satin. As Diana was the goddess of virginity, it was intended to honour Elizabeth as the Virgin Queen. Sir Thomas Benger was her Master of the Revels and he used a troupe of boy actors known as "The Children of St. Pauls." At the end of the masque, the queen and her courtiers would dance. The queen loved to dance so her court dresses had to combine royal dignity with freedom of movement. Often she would practice dancing six or seven galliards every morning with her ladies. The queen also shared her parents' love of music and maintained a choir of forty singers and a company of fifty musicians to entertain at the royal court. But I no longer cared to hear the lute players perform and sing at night. It saddened me to think that if Mark had not been so cruelly struck down then he might have risen to become the Master of the Revels. He had both the talent and the ambition. But he lacked the good fortune to accompany them. So many talented ministers and proud nobles had risen in this court only to fall in their turn. I doubted that anyone would remember the passionate young musician who had once enchanted the court with his playing.

As time passed, I grew accustomed to my new life in the service of Queen Elizabeth. Mistress Ashley regarded me as her own discovery and the four sewing women treated me with great respect. Even Master Smyth came to accept my position as the established royal dressmaker. Perhaps that was because the favour of the queen had so clearly transferred to me. I soon gained the confidence of Mistress Ashley who was her chief Lady in Waiting as well as her Mistress of the Robes. The other longstanding servant of the queen was Mistress Blanche Parry who had been her nurse and was now the Keeper of the Queen's Books. In addition, she was attended by seven

Ladies of the Bedchamber, six maids of honour and four chamberers. The Queen's Gentlewomen were all wellborn and educated ladies who dress the queen, serve her food and entertain her with conversations, card games and reading aloud from the queen's favourite history books. They would also sew the queen's shifts and embroider her sheets and pillowcases in blackwork. Sometimes I would be summoned to instruct them in new designs for purses and cushions. The queen preferred to be served by her familiar attendants who were known as "the old flock of Hatfield."

Being a lady in waiting inevitably involved a great deal of waiting. Mistress Ashley was surprisingly indiscreet and over time she related the history of her service to me. "The queen has led a challenging life in the past and her close servants shared in her difficulties. I was appointed as Lady Governess to the Princess Elizabeth when her brother Prince Edward was born, and I have been part of her household ever since. I taught her reading, writing, languages and needlework. When she was still only a child, she made a sampler for me and an embroidered book cover for her father King Henry. People call her reserved and inscrutable, but a prince cannot afford to wear their heart upon their sleeve. I am the only one who really understands the queen. She suffered greatly from the suspicions of her sister, although she was quite innocent. It has left its mark because she cannot sleep alone at night but must always have an attendant nearby. I have been sent to the Tower three times for her sake, so my loyalty is proven."

"Does the queen ever speak of her mother, Mistress Ashley?"

"Not in public, Mistress Hallows. The late Queen Mary blamed Queen Anne for the sufferings of her mother Queen Catherine, so it was unwise to mention her. And her councillor, Sir William Cecil advised Queen Elizabeth not to stir up the past but let sleeping dogs lie. However, she has not forgotten her. She has brought her mother's relatives at court and promoted them. And she wears a ruby ring on her finger which contains her mother's likeness."

My position as a royal seamstress gave me ample opportunity to observe the character of the young queen. Like her mother, Queen Anne, she was vain about her appearance and determined to present a dazzling image in court. She also had the same need to be the centre of attention and the charisma to fascinate her admirers.

And she showed her vivacious passion for life in her favourite activities of dancing, riding and hunting. She also enjoyed intellectual pursuits including reading, translating and witty conversation. And she had the same dominating will, arrogance and quick temper. Queen Elizabeth had an innate understanding that the royal life of the court was a game to be played. But she was more cautious and wary than her mother. At any time, her sharp intelligence would be deployed to shut down any unwelcome demands but in such a charming way that the petitioner was mollified. To her courtiers she boasted, "I am a lion's cub and inherit many of his qualities." But I saw in her the mother all over again. And I knew what to expect from her as a mistress: the same unreasonable demands for perfection, the expectation for unremitting service and the sarcastic comments if she suspected that a servant might be growing too complacent in their role. On one occasion when the queen had returned from her summer progress she sent for me.

"Mistress Hallows, you must sew the jewelled buttons onto my clothing more securely. A number of them have been lost while on progress."

"I have seen the damage, your Majesty. I fear that zealous citizens have been tearing them off as keepsakes."

"They are too costly to keep replacing, so no more must be lost. I know I can rely on you, Mistress Hallows."

"Yes, your Majesty." But I knew that on the next progress the same thing would happen again. Mistress Ashley witnessed my discomfort and discreetly signalled me to follow her. She led me down a corridor in the palace that led to a locked chamber.

"The queen always dislikes returning to court after her progresses," she confided to me sympathetically. "They give her a respite from the business of state. So she is always ill-humoured on her return."

She unlocked the door and showed me that inside the chamber the table and the floor were stacked with valuable goods of all kinds. "These are all gifts presented to the queen," she informed me. "It is my responsibility to make a catalogue of them. Only the most trusted of the queen's servants could fulfil such a role. It is a great trouble to me, Mistress Hallows, for it is my duty to keep a record and find proper storage so that nothing is lost, stolen or destroyed."

"Who has given these things to the queen, Mistress Ashley?" I enquired. "It is not New Year!"

"The queen is always delighted to receive gifts, especially when they are jewels or items of fine apparel, Mistress Hallows. And she particularly likes sparkling rings which set off her fine white hands. I have placed the best of the gifts on the table so you can see there is a set of white enamelled bracelets from the Marquess of Northampton and a fine fan with a handle set with diamonds from Sir John Puckering. There is also this muff of cloth of gold with seed pearl buttons from Lady Walsingham and a pair of Italian perfumed gloves from the Earl of Oxford. Of course, the givers are all looking for favour, Mistress Hallows."

"If they are bribes, why does the queen accept them, Mistress Ashley?"

"The queen knows the stories of all these fine ladies and gentlemen for she has more knowledge of her kingdom than any of her counsellors. She says that her nobles can easily spare these tokens and that they help to defray the costs of the court. And that the nobility should do its part to support it since they gain so much benefit in return. Take the Dowager Lady Russell. She has just sent the queen a fine hat of white beaver fur set with a pendant pearl. I'll stake my faith that it is worth thirty pounds at least. But this is only the latest in a series of gifts to the queen. She has already sent her a costly gown and petticoat and a set of crimson taffeta curtains for her canopy of state. But it is not prompted by feelings of loyalty or admiration. The greedy old besom wants the queen to grant her the lease of the Dunnington estate. And she thinks that these presents are the best way to get it."

"Surely the queen won't tolerate such corrupt practices, Mistress Ashley?"

"The queen thinks that if there are many petitioners for a favour then the wise course of action is to reward the most generous among them. She is well aware of the Dowager's intentions. And she will lead her a fine dance before she grants her petition."

"But what of her poor subjects who cannot afford to give expensive presents?"

"The queen thinks to benefit the poor too, Mistress Hallows. By encouraging the nobles to contribute to the court, she reduces the burden upon her subjects. And she does not have to go to Parliament to request more taxes. In this way, all play their part in upholding the state. The foreign ambassadors see her dazzling court and send glowing reports about the great wealth and culture of the English queen and her circle. They do not realise that it is but a costly show. And of course, the queen does not keep all these gifts for herself. She retains the most worthy, but most of the offerings of plate are melted down and put into the treasury. I will take a selection of the most splendid gifts over to the queen presently. It will restore her good humour again."

"Is there no better way to fund the costs of the royal court, Mistress Ashley?"

"The queen wishes to rule justly and not seize the estates of her nobles on flimsy pretexts, Mistress Hallows. So she inspires them to compete for her favour instead. And she receives their hospitality whenever she goes on progresses around the kingdom. This reduces the expenses of the royal household while maintaining the glory of the throne. Sometimes I hear the queen muttering that there is no joy in kingship. All these cares are a great trial to her patience. It is why she needs faithful servants like ourselves who support her endeavours without seeking to profit. And the reason that she selects her inner circle with such prudence. There are no end of place seekers who attend the court solely for reward without any thought of return. The queen seeks to promote the most able at her court who will add to its brilliance and do her good service. She does not continue to favour those who simply importune her with more requests."

I understood Mistress Ashley's reasoning about the needs of the state. But I also realised that the queen delighted in receiving the gifts, hospitality and compliments of her nobles. It reinforced her image as Good Queen Bess who was held in love and honour by all her subjects. Some of the queen's petitioners became aware that the best way to gain favour was to discover which presents would be the most acceptable. The Countess of Shrewsbury went so far as to write a letter to Mistress Ashley requesting her advice regarding a suitable gift for the queen. She recommended a cloak in a light blue shade because the queen had no items of that colour in her wardrobe. And she advised her that it should have a border of embroidered pansies as these were the queen's favourite flowers. When this gift arrived at court Mistress Ashley came to summon me to the Privy Chamber. "The queen is of a mind to commission a new dress, Mistress Hallows. And she wishes to discuss it with you herself."

The queen was sitting with a beautiful blue satin cloak draped over her lap. Next to her stood a box of sugared violets to sweeten her breath. She was clearly in an excellent mood and nodded to us as we made our curtsies. "Mistress Hallows, I have just received a gift of this cloak embroidered with pansies from the Countess of Shrewsbury. I should like to have a dress made to complement it and I would be interested to hear your suggestions before I make a decision. Mistress Ashley, you shall write a letter of thanks to my dear friend Bess. Tell her that I have never had a gift that I liked so well."

"Your Majesty might consider a dress of white silk embroidered with sprigs of coloured wildflowers. It would bring a touch of spring into the court during the long winter months to come."

"Indeed, Mistress Hallows, that is a pleasing thought. I have a great fondness for flower designs and this dress shall be a showcase for them. Mistress Ashley, which flowers do you think would look well in such a design?"

"Pansies for certain, your Majesty. But you might also consider pink roses, blue borage and scarlet pimpernels."

"Such a dress will remind the court that the queen is like Persephone, the goddess of springtime. Our Master of the Revels can employ it as a theme for the Eastertide court. In the Greek myths the hero Orpheus brought Persephone from the underworld by the power of his music and she restored harvests and prosperity to the world. And wherever she set her foot, new life would spring up from the barren ground. That is how we tend our realm of England so that it may flourish. Yes, we like it well!"

I was amazed at the great wealth of meaning that could be expressed by the design of a dress. But this was to become typical of Queen Elizabeth. Her special costumes became part of her statecraft and conveyed a message to the court that Elizabeth Tudor represented peace and prosperity.

"You are clear about the requirements for the dress, Mistress Hallows? Good, you may leave us and prepare samplers of the different flowers for our consideration. Mistress Ashley, you may send for the Master of the Revels. I would discuss this masque so that he may devise suitable songs and dances to illustrate the theme of springtime."

I was reminded of her mother, Queen Anne, who also once planned a court masque. But of course, it was not my place to speak to the queen uninvited. Queen Elizabeth was so pleased with the completed dress that she also commissioned a portrait of herself bearing an olive branch as a sign of the peace of the nation. And this also became customary for the queen on significant occasions in her reign. She would order a new portrait of herself wearing an elaborate dress that was filled with symbolic meaning for the viewer. When I saw them, I understood that the queen's gowns were not merely decorative but an expression of her majesty and rule.

The dress of spring flowers was so successful that she made further commissions of gowns with floral motifs for her wardrobe. I made a dress of cloth of silver embroidered all over with roses, pansies, carnations, cowslips and honeysuckle in gold thread and coloured silk thread. And a dress of brown velvet embroidered with a design of pink and green roses and miniature golden suns. I also embroidered a pair of white satin sleeves with roses, daisies and honeysuckle in gold thread, a pair of black satin sleeves with roses, pansies and oak leaves in silver thread and a pair of cloth of gold sleeves with sweet briar, carnations and lilies set with pearls in the centres. In the language of flowers they promoted the attributes of the queen as glorious, fruitful and beautiful. It was my role as the queen's dressmaker to ensure that every item of her clothing represented her royal image as Gloriana, the bringer of wealth and concord.

CHAPTER 17:

THE QUEEN'S SUITORS (1560)

The queen's councillors urged the queen to marry a suitable consort and provide an heir for the sake of the realm. A succession of suitors came to court bringing gifts for the queen and paying her extravagant compliments. She had said that she would only consider a worthy man whom she had seen herself. But time and again her suitors left the court disappointed. I quite understood why the queen did not wish to marry Philip of Spain for he was a most neglectful husband to her sister Mary and highly unpopular among the people. But she also rejected Prince Eric of Sweden, the Duke of Holstein and the Archduke Charles of Austria to the great chagrin of Sir William Cecil who urged her repeatedly to consider the safety of the state and the needs of the succession.

In the meantime, the queen clearly showed her preference for Robert Dudley, her Master of the Horse, who is handsome, charming and witty. He shared her love of riding and dancing and was in constant attendance upon her. She called him "Sweet Robin" and paid him such marked favour that it became the speculation of the court that he was the reason that the queen refused to marry. In 1559 the queen made him a Knight of the Garter. In addition, she granted him the manor of Kew and land in Yorkshire. She also gave him a licence to export woollen cloth free of charge. This provoked considerable envy among the other nobles who regarded him as a self-seeking nobody. It also aroused much speculation among the servants as to whether the queen would follow her heart and marry to please herself rather than pleasing her councillors. One morning when the queen was taking her usual walk in the privy gardens I dared to raise the subject with the Mistress of the Robes.

"You know the queen better than anyone, Mistress Ashley. Is she going to marry Lord Robert?"

Mistress Ashley paused in edging a handkerchief with fine gold thread and sighed. "The queen is blinded by her love for him. She appointed him as her Master of Horse so that they might ride out together. But it is unfitting to her dignity as the queen. I believe that if he had been single, she would have married him already. As it is, she will not have his wife Amy come to court. And now it is reported that she is deathly ill. I fear they intend to marry as soon as she is dead." But this did not come to pass. Amy Robsart was found dead in strange circumstance and her husband Robert was suspected. The scandal was so great that the queen was forced to distance herself and the chance of marrying her favourite was gone. However, she missed his company so much that she once disguised herself as a maid to watch him shoot near Windsor Castle. And she kept all his letters in a locked desk next to her bed.

"Will the queen never marry, Mistress Ashley?"

"I think that she will not, Mistress Hallows, despite all her councillors' pleas. She has seen bad examples, to be sure. Her own father treated all his wives badly. Two of them he executed and two he set aside. Queen Jane Seymour and the Dowager Queen Catherine Parr both died after childbirth. And her sister Mary was little esteemed by her husband Philip. Queen Elizabeth has had the education and upbringing of a prince. She has her father's strong will and she would rule by herself. A husband would take that away from her. I do not think that she would give up her position even for love."

"Then who will inherit the crown from the queen?"

Mistress Ashley lowers her voice. "The succession is not to be discussed. But the queen's next of kin are Catherine and Mary Grey, the younger sisters of Lady Jane Grey who tried to usurp the throne from the late Queen Mary. However, Queen Elizabeth cannot abide either of them. She does not want them here at court." I could see history repeating itself for her sister Mary could barely tolerate the presence of Princess Elizabeth at her court. And in her time, Queen Anne had disliked and mistreated Princess Mary as a rival to her own child.

Queen Elizabeth decided that during the six weeks of Lent that year her ladies in waiting would sew new gowns as Maundy gifts for her to present to twenty poor women. I was delegated to make a best dress as a gift for the occasion and to assist the ladies in their work. Every morning her personal chaplain Father Jonas Wheeler would read to us from the Gospels and the Book of Homilies. Queen Elizabeth was pleased by this display of piety within her household. Sometimes she would enter into deep theological discussions with Father Wheeler. At other times she would reflect upon the morality of the Roman writer Seneca and his advice to princes. "What is true virtue?" she would ask the chaplain. "What is the path of wisdom?" And they would converse together on philosophy to the great admiration of her ladies.

On Easter Sunday the queen and her court attended church and took communion. Afterwards a mystery play was performed in the Great Hall and followed by a lavish feast of roast meats. I listened to the boy actors recite their speeches on the Seven Deadly Sins to the crowded court and I found Master Middleton standing beside me. "A joyful Easter to you, Mistress Hallows," he said. And he gave me a gift of a sachet of lavender embroidered with my initials MH in silver thread. I fastened it by the tassel at my girdle and felt as fine as a noblewoman. I realised that he was growing fond of me. I was flattered that he would seek me out in a court full of young and pretty women. A guild man would be a fine match for a woman of common birth. I thought back to Mark whom I loved to distraction. But he never once gave me a token. My long-ago conversation with Mistress Anne came back to my mind, "If I had a sweetheart he would make me a fairing." She had scorned the idea because the love-struck Henry was sending her jewellery made by his goldsmith. Finally, she had demanded to have the jewels of the queen of England. But she didn't keep them for long.

After that Easter, Master Middleton made it his regular practice to walk with me along the river on Sunday afternoons. He told me of his dreams for the future and I told him of my life as the seamstress to three queens.

"It is an extraordinary tale, Mistress Hallows. It makes my own story sound quite tame. I was orphaned young, but my father and uncle were both broderers. And so, I became the apprentice to my uncle in the guild. It is a hard life but it offers hope and purpose. All of us dream of the day when we can call ourselves a master and profit from our skills."

"Do you plan to make your career at court, Master Middleton?"

"When I had the chance to come to court I thought my fortune was made. But our wages here are no better than in other households. My friends in the guild have told me that there are better prospects in the city than at the court these days. And those who trade do the best of all. I came to court in the reign of Queen Mary and I have saved my wages ever since. When the time is right I will strike out for myself and hazard my fortune."

"It is a good plan, Master Middleton – worthy of a man of ambition."

He smiled. "What is your ambition, Mistress Hallows? Will you serve the queen until your life's end?"

I frowned at his words. I realised that I did not wish to die of old age in the service of the queen. But what alternative was there?

"You do not answer, Mistress?"

I collected myself. "It is different for a woman, Master Middleton. A single woman can either take service or live as a poor spinster."

"But a married woman may partner her husband in business. And if she is widowed she may oversee it by herself."

"I have grown wary of ambition, Master Middleton. I have seen much of it at court and it leads to misery rather than happiness."

"Perhaps because the ambition was too great. I believe that a moderate ambition may be fostered into prosperity and contentment. This is the way of a guild man and his craft. It is a journey made of patient labour and slow reward. But those who persevere often reach success."

I pondered his words. "Yes, a small ambition is the safe course to take. Especially at court where the rash and imprudent think that royal favour will raise them to great heights. But too often it leads to tragedy."

"Of whom do you speak, Mistress Hallows?"

"Of a lady who conquered the heart of a king only to find that it was fickle and vengeful at the last. And of a servant who thought that his talents would raise him above his degree, but it brought enmity instead."

"If he had belonged to a guild then he would have had protection. A master craftsman can rise above his birth by virtue of his talent."

"The court can be perilous to all, Master Middleton. Commoners and nobles, men and women alike – to all those with over-great ambition. And so a small ambition is a prudent course to take."

"And what is yours, Mistress Hallows?"

"It is to serve well and deserve a pension when I am old."

"I think your ambition is too small, Mistress Hallows. Did you never dream of anything more in your youth?"

I shook my head. "I spent my youth in the service of the Boleyn's. And when they fell from favour at court I was fortunate to survive it. So I came to see dreams as a folly."

"You were unfortunate, Mistress Hallows. But you are not to blame and should not give up your hopes because of the folly of others."

Perhaps I should not after all. Neither Queen Anne nor Queen Elizabeth considered my dreams. But the Lady Anne of Cleves had thought of my happiness. I realised that I was not much of a talker. My father had been a taciturn man who regarded idle chatter as an interruption of profitable work. And sewing is a demanding task which requires total concentration. When I began in service I was directed to listen to my elders and betters. And at the royal court Mistress Harvey had not tolerated talk among the seamstresses. Looking back, my youth was spent in a world of silence as I had practised my skills. And I unconsciously took on the role of a listener – to Mistress Anne and to Mark. I never gained their ease in conversation nor their flair for witticisms. All my communication was expressed through my craft. Maybe this was what Master Middleton had meant by the years of sacrifice required of apprentices in order to attain mastery. Perhaps I should shake off that discipline and reap my reward. I could live off my craft and choose my own future. I only needed the courage to take it for myself. At Whitsun I gave Master Middleton a sweet bag embroidered with an intertwining pattern of vines. He smiled when he saw it.

"Now we are troth-plighted, are we not Mistress Hallows?"

"Call me Margery now," I said to him.

"And I am William."

CHAPTER 18:

THE QUEEN'S WARDROBE (1562)

In 1562 Queen Elizabeth nearly died from an attack of smallpox at Hampton Court Palace. She requested that in the event of her death Sir Robert Dudley should be appointed as Protector of the Realm, which greatly alarmed her adviser Sir William Cecil. But to the vast relief of everyone, the queen made a good recovery. However, the queen made Sir Robert a Privy Counsellor and the following year she gave him Kenilworth Castle in Warwickshire. And finally, she granted him the title of Earl of Leicester. Naturally, this caused much envy and matters came to a head at a tennis match when the Duke of Norfolk threatened to strike him in the face with his racquet. The crisis of the queen's illness led her councillor Sir William Cecil to renew the question of her marriage. But she declared that she would rather be a beggarwoman and single than a queen and married. A delegation from Parliament came to Whitehall Palace and begged the queen to marry. In response, she held up the Coronation ring and said, "I am already bound to a husband, which is the kingdom of England."

Queen Elizabeth's devoted lady in waiting Mary Sidney nursed her throughout her illness, but then caught smallpox so badly herself that she was dreadfully scarred and retired from the court. The queen's illness had less drastic effects but her appearance was never the same. She became reliant upon cosmetics to create a smooth completion. And she compensated for the loss of her beauty by paying more attention to her dress. It would take two hours every morning for her ladies to complete her toilette. She changed her views considerably about her dress style and abandoned dark and sober colours. She would delight in wearing vivid colours, while her ladies were restricted to wearing black and white. On one occasion, her lady in waiting Mary Howard presented herself at court wearing a splendid velvet dress decorated with gold and pearls. But the queen told her that it was much too fine and forbade her from wearing it.

Over the course of her reign Queen Elizabeth accumulated a vast royal wardrobe of hundreds of dresses of all colours. Court dress for ladies was marked by square necklines, tight bodices, bell-shaped skirts, full sleeves and large ruffs. The fashion developed into farthingale skirts, puffed sleeves and cartwheel ruffs. The skirts of the ladies in waiting became so wide that there wasn't enough room for them to sit on their benches at mealtimes. The bodices and sleeves of the dresses were highly decorated with designs of flowers, insects and animals in coloured silks and gold and silver thread. This style of elaborate embroidery became my speciality as the dressmaker to the queen. The court artists would paint portraits of the queen wearing her best costumes as an image of the glory of the Tudor house. They portrayed her in splendid dresses of silk, satin and cloth of gold studded with white pearls as symbols of virginity. They were embroidered with intertwining patterns of roses, carnations and pansies and adorned with fine coloured jewels. I would undertake these special commissions with the assistance of the sewing women and the queen's embroiderers.

At Candlemas 1564 Mistress Ashley summoned me urgently to the Privy Chamber where Queen Elizabeth was deep in discussion with Sir William Cecil. I see that the queen's goldsmith Robert Brandon, his young apprentice Nicholas Hilliard and the queen's silk woman Alice Montague are already in attendance. As we waited respectfully for permission to approach the queen Mistress Ashley explained the reason for our summons.

"There is going to be an important embassy at court," she whispered. "A new ambassador Guzman de Silva has been appointed and will soon be on his way here. The queen has just received the news from Spain. Relations with Spain have not always been easy and the queen wants to make a good impression on the new ambassador. She is planning a new dress for the occasion and it must be ready on time."

Finally, the queen beckoned us to come forward and we made our reverences. "Mistress Ashley, I have it in mind to wear a dress of gold satin embroidered with a design of red roses with intertwining gold stems and interspaced with gold and ruby spangles on the bodice and the sleeves. The ornaments and the embroidery must match. The colours must be as close as possible. This is why I have summoned the masters of the craft here. Master Brandon, I wish you to bring me an example of the spangle the day after tomorrow. I shall probably require three dozen for the bodice and the sleeves, so your apprentice may assist you. Mistress Smythe, I wish you to bring me all your spools of gold threads and red silk threads so that I may make a comparison. And then Mistress Hallows, I shall want to see a sample of the worked design for my approval. On this occasion, I wish to fully realise my vision and I do not want to be disappointed by an inferior selection of threads."

She turned to face Sir William with a triumphant smile. "This will impress the new Spanish ambassador and his entourage with the wealth and might of England. It is my intention that every report that goes out will express the splendour of our court and the glory of her queen. Splendour equates to might in the minds of my brother monarchs."

"It is a dangerous strategem to rely upon a court masque for the defence of the realm, your Majesty."

Her smile faded. "Diplomacy is all a masque, Sir William. Why do you think I enjoy it so much?"

"Masques or diplomacy, your Majesty?"

"They both serve the same purpose, Sir William – to humble the minds of the proud and dazzle the eyes of the covetous and to ensure the peace of the realm. I am the greatest peacemaker in Europe and my court is a celebration of the peaceful arts."

"Such a policy may be misunderstood as a fear of war, your Majesty. And these court costumes are a considerable expense. Do you not have hundreds of fine dresses in your wardrobe and numerous jewels in your coffers already?"

"Indeed, my lord, there is no need for costly war when we can use subtle persuasion instead. I had rather spend on lavish gifts and hospitality than spend the lives of my countrymen. I am not ignorant of what becomes a king."

"Your father's wars made the nation feared and it pleased the nobles to demonstrate their prowess on the battlefield, your Majesty."

"My father's wars were ruinous and those of my sister Mary were disastrous, Sir William. Monarchs who are over-fond of war end by beggaring their nation. As you know, we spend our days in endless correspondence, audiences and receptions to build friendships and win allies abroad. Our nobility understand the folly of being drawn into foreign wars which only serve the interests of other powers."

She signalled us to depart and we withdrew. I was astounded at the revelation of the queen's mind which is usually so guarded and impenetrable. Mistress Ashley glanced at me with pride. "Now you see her greatness, Mistress Margery. These commissions are part of her governance and you can take satisfaction in making your own contribution to it." I had to agree that Queen Elizabeth had a higher vision than her mother Queen Anne who had aspired to be the arbiter of fashion at the court, but not the architect of the royal image.

Queen Elizabeth was a demanding mistress who regarded marriage as an inferior option to royal service for her ladies. She would often exhort all her women to remain in the virgin state and ask them if they ever thought about marriage. Since they were aware of the queen's opinion they were astute enough to reject the idea which greatly pleased her. However, this question proved disastrous for one newcomer to court who innocently informed the queen that there was a man she loved and she hoped that her father would give consent to their marriage. "You are a foolish young girl," snapped the queen. "Your father may give you permission, but I never shall." Poor Mary Arundell was left heartbroken for she had lost the chance for marriage to the man of her choice. As a result of the queen's prejudice against marriage her ladies were afraid to seek her permission and sometimes got married in secret. In 1560 Lady Catherine Grey had contracted a secret marriage with Edward Seymour and when it was discovered the queen sent them both to the Tower.

CHAPTER 19:

Farewell to Court (1565)

At the beginning of 1565 William was made a full liveryman in his guild and he was permitted to marry. He told me his good news with great delight. "Now I have the right to speak. I am not a man of many words, Margery, but I have a true heart. And I have wanted you to be my wife ever since the first Christmas that you came to court. Will you marry me?"

"Yes, William. I can think of no better happiness than to be your wife."

"I would give up this royal livery and be my own master. It is better than being a servant, even the servant of a queen."

I could hardly imagine a life outside service. It seemed too good to be true.

"We'll leave the court and set up our own business right here in London. The salaries of the court servants haven't increased since the time of old Henry. We can do much better on our own. There are plenty of prosperous merchants and their wives who want to dress in the fashion of the court. You can outfit the women and I will tailor the men."

"The queen won't like it if we get married and leave, William."

"It doesn't matter if she likes it or not, Margery. We're not the nobility and she can't interfere with us as she does with her ladies in waiting. We'll leave as soon as I have found a suitable property. The guild will assist us in establishing our business."

But in the summer of 1565 Mistress Ashley unexpectedly died leaving Queen Elizabeth quite inconsolable. She was sixty-three years old and had served the queen for thirty years. The queen gave the position of Mistress of the Robes to Lady Dorothy Stafford and the post of Chief Gentlewoman to Mistress Blanche Parry. She sent for me to attend her in her Privy Chamber. "Mistress Hallows, from now on Lady Stafford will be in charge of the seamstresses," she said complacently. "You will be her assistant with special responsibility for making all my costumes."

I noticed that there was no mention of an increased salary. "It is most kind of your Majesty, but I will be leaving the court soon," I replied. "Master Middleton and I are getting married and we want to set up our own household together."

Her eyes narrowed instantly at my words. "What are you saying? You want to marry and leave my service? I forbid you even to think of such a thing! Where is your loyalty and your duty to me as your sovereign? You are needed here, both of you are needed. Especially after the loss of our beloved Mistress Ashley. How can you suppose that you could go at such a time?"

Lady Stafford cleared her throat. "I am sure, your Majesty, that Mistress Hallows will realise that her place is here with you. And there is no reason why she and Master Middleton should not marry and continue their service."

But the queen was in no mood for compromise. "I have not said so, Lady Stafford. My permission must be requested before any of my household can marry. And my permission is refused. I do not hold with divided loyalties. I have told you of the new arrangements for the wardrobe, Mistress Hallows, so now you may go. And put all foolish thoughts of marriage from your mind."

I curtsied and left the queen's presence as quickly as I could. If only I had asked Mistress Ashley to intercede for me with the queen. She would have known how best to persuade her. Now it is too late. I went in search of William and told him the terrible news. He was furious to hear of the queen's high-handedness.

"We may be her servants, but we are not in bondage. We are of age and have the means to marry. And we have every right to leave the court if we choose. I am a guild master and not some lackey."

"The queen is very angry with us at present. It would be dangerous to cross her.

We must make a plan, William. Perhaps you could find someone from the guild to take your place here. And maybe we could ask one of her advisers to speak for us."

"The only councillor she will heed is Sir William Cecil. And he is not going to concern himself about the queen's wardrobe."

"Let me speak to Lady Stafford. She was sympathetic to the idea of our marriage. Perhaps she can soften the queen."

But Lady Stafford refused to discuss the subject with me. "The queen has made her feelings quite clear on the matter, Mistress Hallows. I counsel you to follow her wishes and forget such a notion. You are fortunate to have this good position at court and to serve her as your mistress."

I thought back resentfully to Lady Anne of Cleves who had offered to find a match for me in her household. "Like mother, like daughter," I thought to myself. Neither Queen Anne nor Queen Elizabeth gave any thought to the good of their servants. They only cared about their own convenience.

But William refused to be deterred. "The queen will have to manage without us, Margery. I have known other royal servants to prosper well on their own account. I have found a suitable property to rent near to the Broderer's Hall. As a master I can train my own apprentices and you can supervise a team of sewing women. In a few years' time we will live as well as any merchant in the city."

I know it is true. I had known Mistress Joan Wilkinson who had been the silk woman to Queen Anne. Her husband was a London mercer and they grew rich from the trade in luxury goods from Europe. Just one consignment of fine fabric would bring a greater profit than both our yearly salaries at court. And the proceeds from outfitting the merchant class would make us a fortune once it was known that we had been the dressmakers to the queen. I reminded myself that my father would have thought just the same as William.

I sought out Mistress Ashley's widowed husband John Ashley, the Master of the Jewel House, and asked his advice.

"How can we persuade the queen to let us marry, Master Ashley?"

"That is not an easy matter as you know, Mistress Hallows," he replied sombrely. "Once the queen is suited with her servants, then she is most reluctant to part with them. If my poor wife were here then she would have thought of a way, but now I fear the queen will be even more unwilling."

"But some of the queen's servants marry, do they not?"

"She agreed to our marriage, but then she was still a young woman and not yet the queen. It is best in such a matter to find an intercessor to speak to the queen, but I don't know who could manage to persuade her. She will not want to lose two valuable servants from her wardrobe. I am sorry that I cannot be of better assistance to you."

I was downcast and reported back to William that even the queen's longstanding servants did not know how to help us. The queen's prejudice against marriage was too well known. The only point in our favour is that neither of us can be considered too young. If we were to approach one of the queen's chaplains without her permission it would only bring trouble down upon them. However, William was resourceful and sought out the chaplain to the guild. He agreed to marry us at the church of St Benet's, Paul's Wharf. William got permission to visit the Broderer's Hall that day and told me to excuse myself to Lady Stafford so that I might accompany him. I was disappointed that I did not have the opportunity to make a new wedding dress, but my best dress would have to suffice for the occasion. William found a boatman to take us up the river to the watergate of Baynard's Castle and from there we made our way to St Benet's church. The chaplain was waiting for us at the door with several members of the guild. There we clasped our hands and said our vows of matrimony and William placed his ring upon my finger. After the service we made our way to the Broderer's Hall and dined with our guests. And then William took me to see our new home and we went up to our bedchamber together where we become irrevocably man and wife.

The next day we returned to the Palace of Whitehall. William accompanied me to see Lady Stafford. "Where have you been all this time, Margery? No one could find you anywhere."

"Yesterday was my wedding day, Lady Stafford," I informed her proudly. "William and I were married by the chaplain of his guild."

"I shall have to tell the queen what you have done," she said ominously. "I cannot answer for the consequences." She departed and then returned looking pale. "The queen commands that you come to her at once." We made our way to the Privy Chamber.

As soon as she sets eyes on us the queen began to abuse us. "False servants! I refused to give permission for your marriage and you have defied me. Who are you to set my will at naught? Better born persons than you lie in prison for their secret marriages. And so shall both of you."

"Your Majesty," I replied with a calmness that astonished her. "I am not only your true servant but I served your mother Queen Anne faithfully until her death. And when I was still only a girl I carried your mother's last message to you and told it to her chaplain Father Parker under the seal of confession. If this had been discovered then I could have died with her."

She became very quiet and rubbed the ruby ring upon her finger. "Do you presume to speak to me of my mother? What is this message?"

I drew a deep breath sensing the great danger of this moment. "Your mother asked me to convey this message to you as my last service to her, "Tell her that as I sit here in the Tower all my thoughts are of her. And though I die condemned, yet I was a loyal and faithful wife to the king and his undoubted Queen. And she is his true daughter and I commend her to show herself as his most affectionate and dutiful subject. And although the king will never acknowledge me, yet my friends who are known to Reverend Parker know the truth..."

"No more of this," declared the queen. "Where did you hear those words? You listened while others gossiped I'll be bound."

"I heard them from your mother, Queen Anne, when I took a set of clothes to her in the Tower," I replied. "And I told them to Father Parker, but to no other soul on earth until this day."

"This tale shall be proven or else you will go to the Tower for daring to speak of such things," she stormed. "Go from my sight. I can endure no more this day."

William and I made our courtesies and withdrew. We were greatly alarmed by the sight of the queen in such a rage. What would become of us? William took my hand. "You are as bold as a lion, Mistress Middleton. I am glad to have you as my wife."

The next morning, we are summoned to the presence of Sir William Cecil. "The queen is incensed," he warns us. "She would have had you imprisoned already, but I persuaded her to let me speak first to Archbishop Parker. It is unwise to speak to the queen of her mother."

"I spoke only the truth, Sir William. I am an old servant of the Boleyn's and I have married a worthy man. There is no harm in that."

"There is a time for everything, Mistress Middleton. I am surprised that service to three queens did not teach you to be more circumspect. I had thought you a sensible woman, not like these giddy maids of honour."

"Queen Anne and the Lady Anne of Cleves would not have stood in the way of my marriage, Sir William."

"Well, now the fat is in the fire. You can only hope that Archbishop Parker can smooth things over. The queen sets great store upon his opinions. Otherwise, you will have only yourselves to blame. Whatever the right of it, the queen is the queen and she will not brook defiance."

We spent an anxious week awaiting the outcome of events. Then Sir William sent for us again. "Well, you are most fortunate, Mistress Middleton. The archbishop remembered you and commended your service to the queen. Moreover, he thought you ought to be rewarded for your courage. And he reminded her that the honourable state of marriage is not to be despised. So he has acted the part of your friend. The queen will not see you, but she will allow you both to leave her service and she has agreed to pay you your salaries. So you have nothing of which to complain."

"We are most grateful to you, Sir William," I replied. "I pray you tell the queen that we are thankful for her great kindness to us."

He handed William a red purse. "I wish you good fortune in your venture, Master Middleton. I am sure that you will thrive in the city."

William made the arrangements to convey our chests to our home in the city. His guild assisted him to buy goods and find clients and within a year we had sufficient customers to justify taking on our first apprentice. William undertook trading expeditions to Calais, Paris and Antwerp and set himself up as a successful mercer. In time we fulfilled his ambition to supervise a team of skilled broderers who specialised in outfitting those who aspire to a career at court. We purchased our house and we dined and dressed just as finely as a city merchant. There was even talk of William becoming an alderman of the city. I found myself wishing that my father had lived to see this day. I looked back over my life and wondered how I reached this place from my humble beginnings on the farm. I am glad that I escaped the dangers of the royal court for the lesser risks of a city business. I have known two ambitious men at court of whom one rose high while the other fell low. And I cannot attribute this only to chance but to prudence. I saw that the Lady Anne of Cleves was right for I have found true happiness with a man of my own mind. I no longer grieve for Mark, but I have not forgotten him. And every year on 17th May I unwrap the bindings of his lute and remember the songs of my youth and the one who sang them.

"Who list his wealth and ease retain,
Himself let him unknown contain.
Press not too fast in at that gate
Where the return stands by disdain,
For sure, *circa Regna tonat*.

The high mountains are blasted oft
When the low valley is mild and soft.
Fortune with Health stands at debate.
The fall is grievous from aloft.
And sure, circa Regna tonat.

These bloody days have broken my heart.
My lust, my youth did them depart,
And blind desire of estate.
Who hastes to climb seeks to revert.
Of truth, circa Regna tonat."

Thomas Wyatt.

THE END

Printed in Great Britain
by Amazon

24590626R00067